The Black Book
[DIARY OF A TEENAGE STUD]
VOL. III

Run, Jonah, Run

JONAH BLACK

AVON BOOKS
An Imprint of HarperCollins Publishers

The Black Book [Diary of a Teenage Stud], Vol. III:
Run, Jonah, Run

Copyright © 2001 by 17th Street Productions,
an Alloy Online, Inc. company.

Cover Photograph from Tony Stone
Design by Russell Gordon

Printed in the United States of America.

For information address
HarperCollins Children's Books, a division of
HarperCollins Publishers, 1350 Avenue of the Americas,
New York, NY 10019.

 Produced by 17th Street Productions,
an Alloy Online, Inc. company
151 West 26th Street, New York, NY 10001

Library of Congress Catalog Card Number: 2001116876
ISBN 0-06-440800-0

First Avon edition, 2001

AVON TRADEMARK REG. U.S. PAT. OFF.
AND IN OTHER COUNTRIES,
MARCA REGISTRADA, HECHO EN U.S.A.

Visit us on the World Wide Web!
www.harperteen.com

Run, Jonah, Run

Nov. 28, 7:30 P.M.

I just took my own picture with a Polaroid camera. The last photograph of me before I lose my virginity. I sat on the bed and held the camera at arm's length and smiled. The flash turned my eyes all red, so now I have this Last Picture of Jonah as a Virgin, and I look like some kind of werewolf. Tonight, when I get back from Posie's, maybe I'll take another photograph and compare the two.

I'm sitting in my room, listening to Mom's radio show, *Pillow Talk*, on WOMN-FM. I have to admit it's become an obsession. It's like a horror movie where you cover your eyes, but then you spread your fingers and peek because you have to see what happens next.

All these kids are calling Mom up and asking her

these crazy questions. *I'm a fifteen-year-old girl and whenever I kiss a guy I get the hiccups. Is this normal?* Or, *I'm a sixteen-year-old boy and I like to read* Vogue *and* Mademoiselle. *Is this normal?* Or, *I'm a seventeen-year-old boy and I don't want to touch a girl unless I'm listening to Jay-Z. Is this normal?* No matter what questions get asked, Mom always answers the same thing: *Tell me—are you being nice to yourself?*

I almost called up Mom myself. Here's what I'd say: *"Doctor" Black, I'm this seventeen-year-old guy who was held back a year in school for completely unfair reasons and now I'm in the eleventh grade all over again while my friends are all seniors, and I'm just about to sleep with the perfect girl who's been my friend since I was ten, except that I can't stop thinking about this kind of mystery girl I know from this boarding school in Pennsylvania I used to go to. Is this normal?*

I could even answer her next question: *And no, I'm not being nice to myself. I think I'm being nice to everybody else, though. Does that count?*

What does "being nice to yourself" mean exactly anyway?

I think I'm going to jump on my bike and head over to Posie's house pretty soon. I've got the flowers I bought from Rite Aid, and the condoms I bought a couple weeks ago. I even hav

───── ■ ─────

Okay, at that exact second the phone rang.

Somehow I knew it was Sophie from the sound of the ring. I can't explain this except that as I walked to the kitchen to pick up the cordless, I had absolutely no doubt about who it was.

"Hi? Jonah?" I could see her so clearly, I could almost smell her shampoo. It was amazing that she could be calling me in Pompano Beach, Florida, all the way from Bryn Mawr, Pennsylvania, and have it sound like she was in the same room. In the background, I could hear the sound of the traffic on Lancaster Pike, which is this big road in front of Masthead Academy. I knew she was standing at the pay phone outside Webber Hall, which is the administration building. I wondered why she hadn't used the phone in the hallway of the girls' dorm, but maybe she wanted privacy when she talked to me. I liked that.

"Sophie?" I said. "How are you?"

"I'm—okay. I guess," she said. "Kind of weird, actually."

"Really? Are you all right?" I asked. She sounded strange.

"Yeah. I'm all right. It's just weird, you know? I miss you."

3

"I miss you, too, Sophie. How's everything at Masthead?"

"Oh, Jonah, you know what it's like here. It's lunatic city. Except it's worse because everybody's under all this pressure, waiting to find out where we got into college."

"Where did you apply?" I asked her.

There was this big pause.

"Uh, you don't have to tell me if you don't want to," I said.

"No, it's okay. I applied to a bunch of schools. Stanford, in California. Tulane, in New Orleans. Carleton, in Minnesota. The University of Colorado. And the University of Central Florida."

"UCF? You applied to UCF?" I said. It's not exactly the greatest school in the world. It's good for partying, though, I guess.

"Yeah, well. It's good to keep your options open, right?" Sophie said.

"I guess."

"Where are you applying, Jonah?"

I wanted to come up with some great lie for her, but I couldn't. "I'm not applying to schools," I said. "I'm back in eleventh grade. Remember?"

"Oh, right," Sophie said. I could almost feel myself shrinking in her eyes. "Because of the . . . the thing last spring."

I loved the way she called it "the thing." *Yeah, because I drove a car through the wall of a motel by accident. Because I was trying to save you, Sophie. Because I was trying to keep you from having to sleep with my stupid ex-roommate Sullivan the Giant. Because I got expelled and had to come back to live at my mom's house in Pompano Beach. Because I'm a loser!*

"Orlando's not far from where you are, is it, Jonah?" she said.

"Well, it's a couple of hours away, actually."

"Oh." She sounded disappointed. "Well, anyway. That's part of why I'm coming down there. To check out the campus. That, plus I'm taking this vacation with my parents." There was a little pause. "Did you still want to try to get together? When I come down?"

"Yeah," I said. "I'd like that." Then I thought about Posie, less than a mile away, waiting for me to come over for our Big Night. I didn't even feel that guilty. What's wrong with me?

"We're staying at the Porpoise," Sophie told me. The schedule is, I'm at Masthead until the nineteenth. Then I'm flying up to Maine to spend Christmas with my family in Kennebunkport. Then on the twenty-sixth we're all going down to Disney World. Why don't we try to meet then?"

"Okay. I have to try to figure this out, though. I need a good excuse for why I'd go to Orlando for a couple days," I said.

"Well, you could tell them you're meeting a girl at some hotel. How do you think that would go over with your mother?" Sophie joked.

I could still hear my mother's voice on the radio. "Bup, bup, bup," she said, interrupting some caller. "It doesn't matter what you *think*! What's important is how you *feel*!"

"I don't know how it would go over," I said. "It's none of her business, my—you know. Love life."

There was another long pause. I pictured Sophie standing there outside in the cold. The Masthead senior class was probably doing its annual Christmas tree sale out in the parking lot.

"I'm not going to tell my parents, either," Sophie said.

"Tell them what?"

"That I'm going to see you."

I couldn't think of anything to say in response. I just let those words echo all over my body.

"Hey, Jonah, there's something else I want to tell you," Sophie said.

"What?"

"About your roommate? I mean, ex-roommate?" she said.

6

"Sullivan?"

"I never slept with him, Jonah. I wanted you to know. I haven't slept with anybody, actually. I've been waiting."

"Me too," I whispered. But I was about to go over to my friend Posie's house and sleep with her. I felt like I was going to snap in two. I couldn't figure out which girl I was being unfaithful to.

"I'm glad," Sophie said. In the background, I heard a car horn honk. "Uh-oh, gotta go," she said hurriedly. "I'll call you again, okay? Why don't you book a room at the Porpoise from the twenty-seventh to the thirtieth? Then we can just see each other whenever I can get away from my parents. Okay? I'll talk to you later. 'Bye!"

And then she hung up.

Now I'm sitting on my bed writing this down in my notebook. I'm wearing my best black shirt and this pair of jeans that I know Posie likes. I'm looking at this photograph of myself with red werewolf eyes. I'm holding a bouquet of flowers.

And all I can think about is going to Disney World to stay at a hotel with Sophie.

Nov. 29, 12:30 A.M.

Okay, so it was a disaster. I went over there and Actually, you know what? This is too depressing

7

to write right now. I'm going to bed. I'll give this another shot tomorrow. For now let me just write down the three magic words for tonight: STUPID STUPID STUPID.

Nov. 29

It's Saturday morning, almost eleven A.M., but I'm still in my room. I can't make myself face the world today. I just feel like sitting here listening to music and writing. I'm listening to Radiohead, which is perfect for my mood. Seriously morbid.

All right, now for the exciting details of Jonah's Big Disaster.

Maybe if I write this quickly it won't be so horrible. Maybe not.

I went over to Posie's and man did she have the place all set up. She had a fire going in her parents' fireplace. It's one of those fake gas fireplaces, but it was nice anyway. She'd made this whole dinner for us—a roasted chicken—and she'd got out her parents' good china and silverware. As it turned out, her folks had decided to stay overnight in Lauderdale. Plus, her little sister, Caitlin, had gone out with her friends to the Muvico, so we had the whole place to ourselves. Caitlin was going to be back around eleven, but that was all right. Caitlin was cool with me and Posie being together.

Anyway, we started to eat this chicken and Posie had even opened a bottle of white wine. It was sweet and went right to my brain and I was just sitting there in this kind of haze.

Posie was wearing a black lacy top that kind of clung to her, and it was all I could do to keep my eyes on her face. She also had on a short khaki skirt that showed off her legs. Maybe sometime I should write a whole thing about Posie's legs, because they are like, this natural wonder, like the Grand Canyon or Mount Rushmore. She has this crazy tan from being out on the ocean so much, and she has really strong muscles from surfing, too. But she doesn't have those giant weight-lifter legs that a lot of girls get when they work out. They just seem strong and smooth and brown and amazing.

Of course I couldn't see her legs under the tablecloth, but I knew they were there.

Posie asked me if I like chicken.

"I like this one a lot," I said.

"What's your favorite part of the chicken?" she said.

"I'm not sure."

And then she said, "You know, what I like is the thigh. I love the dark meat on the thigh. It's so delicate and moist. What do you think, Jonah? Do you like the thigh?"

I laughed. "Yeah, Posie, the thigh is all right."

Then she said, "But sometimes I like the breast better. The white meat on the breast is kind of soft and delicious, too. I don't know. It's kind of hard to choose between the breast and the thigh, isn't it, Jonah?"

Posie is such a nut. I loved how she was teasing me with that whole chicken thing. It felt so great, just sitting there being seduced by her.

"There are a lot of parts to admire in a chicken, aren't there?" I said, grinning at her.

"Mmm-hmm," Posie said. Then she laughed. "Hey, Jonah," she said. "Why don't you come over here and admire *my* parts?"

So I stood up and walked over to her and kissed her brains out.

After a while, Posie took me by the hand and we went into her bedroom and I lay down on her bed, the same bed I'd been sitting on since we were kids, only now it felt like something else, like a launch pad for a rocket over at Cape Canaveral.

"I'm going to be right back," she said, and went into the bathroom. I took off all my clothes and got under the covers and waited for her. I couldn't believe it was going to happen. I suddenly remembered about the condoms, so I got up and got my wallet out of my pants pocket and got the Trojan and put it on Posie's bedside table. Then I got back into bed again. Just in time for Posie to come out of the bathroom wearing absolutely nothing. She went over to her bureau and lit a candle and then turned off all the rest of the lights in the room and lay down next to me and kissed me.

I put my arms around her and I felt like I had super powers. Like I was "The One." Keanu Reeves in *The Matrix*.

"I love you, Jonah," Posie whispered. "Take off your clothes."

"I love you, too, Sophie," I said.

I heard it as I said it, but I didn't realize how horrible it was until a second later when I felt the change in Posie. It was like someone had thrown freezing water on her.

"Sophie?" she said. "You called me *Sophie*?"

"No, I didn't," I said.

"You did!" Posie cried. "For crying out loud, Jonah!"

———— ■ ————

"I'm sorry," I said. "It was just a mistake. It was just something I—"

I was blushing hard, and stuttering. Posie was staring at me as though she suddenly saw something in me she hadn't seen before.

"You really do love her, don't you?"

"Posie, this is stupid, I don't even—"

"Jonah, come on. We've known each other too long to lie to each other. Tell me the truth. Do you still love her?"

I didn't answer right away, which in a way was worse than anything I could have said.

"Oh, my God," Posie said, leaning back against the pillow. "Oh, Jonah."

"I don't love her," I said. "Really, it was just a mistake."

"Shut up," Posie said, and she hit me in the chest. She got out of bed suddenly and turned on the lights and blew out the candle and went into the bathroom.

I lay back in the bed for a moment feeling like the biggest creep in the world. I couldn't believe it! Here I was, about to have sex for the first time with my best friend Posie, this totally amazing girl, and I screwed it up by calling her Sophie. This mystery girl I hardly even know. What's wrong with me? Am I totally stupid?

YES YOU INCREDIBLE MORON YOU'RE STUPID.

After a while I got up and I put my boxers and jeans back on, although not my shirt, and I went to the bathroom door.

"Posie?" I said.

"Leave me alone," she said.

"I'm sorry," I said. "Can you come out? So we can talk?"

"I'll come out in a second," Posie said, and I could tell from her voice she was crying, and that she was embarrassed that she was crying and was trying to both cover it up and stop.

"Okay," I said. I went back to her bed and lay there for a while. I picked up a magazine by her bed—*WAHINE: The Girls' Guide to Surfing and Watersports*, and I read it for a while without understanding any of the words. Although I noticed that a lot of the girls in the magazine were pretty incredible-looking.

At last, Posie came out of the bathroom. She'd put her clothes back on, and I felt bad that I hadn't put my shirt on. She sat next to me on the bed, and I put the magazine down on top of the still-unwrapped condom on her bedside table.

"Jonah, what are we going to do?" She took my hand, and for a second I looked at it. Posie has cool fingers—long and slender and brown.

"I don't know," I said.

"Stop grunting at me," she said. "You've been grunting at me all night. I need you to talk and tell me what's going on in that head of yours."

"I don't know what's going on in my head. Honestly. That's why I'm being so weird. I mean, I know I love you, Posie."

"I love you, too, Jonah." She sighed, and let go of my hand. "But tell me. How are you going to get her out of your system?"

"She *is* out of my system. Honestly." Even as I said it, though, I knew I was lying. I knew Posie could tell, too.

"She isn't," she said.

"Come on, Posie," I pleaded. "I just made a mistake. It's not that big a deal."

"Jonah," she said, and her voice sounded tired. "I don't care if you're still obsessed with this chick. But you have to at least admit it. You have to get your head clear. Do you want to be with me or her?"

"I want to be with you. Of course I want to be with you." I was saying it, but I wasn't sure I meant it. "I mean, how could I be with her? She goes to school in Pennsylvania, and she lives in Maine."

Again, I realized I'd made a mistake even as I said it. Posie answered me in this very small voice. "So—you'd be with her if she lived near here? If she lived in Florida?"

"No," I said. "I don't know. Of course not."

"Jonah, what is it with her? What happened up in Pennsylvania? You never told me the whole story."

I really didn't want to go into it just then. All I really wanted was for Posie to take her clothes off again and for us to have sex. But I guess it was starting to become clear to me that that wasn't going to happen. It might not ever happen.

And then I realized I was talking to my oldest friend. Posie is the one person in the world, besides Thorne, that I *could* talk to about it.

So I told her the story of Sophie. How I'd always been obsessed with her, but I wasn't sure she even knew I was alive. Like I'd see her standing by herself on a snowy day, just looking out over the cornfield behind the football field. Or she'd be up in the bell tower, looking down on everybody going past. She had this kind of distant serenity or something, like she was removed from everything, just watching. Really watching. It was the way I felt about the world sometimes, and I had this feeling that Sophie, whoever she was, maybe saw the world the same way I did.

Then I told Posie about my awful roommate Sullivan the Giant, whose father was a trustee at Masthead, and how Sullivan had access to everybody's files, and how he blackmailed girls into going out with him. He went through the alphabet, hooking up with each girl in the class. By the spring he'd gotten around to Sophie, whose last name starts with an O. I told Posie how my friend Betsy Donnelly and I made a plan to stop him, except that there was kind of a weak link in the plan, which was that I can't drive all that well. Instead of going over to this motel to rescue Sophie from Sullivan, I drove the dean's Peugeot through the wall of the motel and got expelled. I saved Sophie though. She ran off into the night before Sullivan got to her.

"What did Sullivan know about her?" Posie asked me.

"What?"

"You said this guy Sullivan had information he could use against all these girls, to make them go out with him. So what did he find out about Sophie that was so terrible she'd rather hook up with Sullivan in some motel than have everybody know?"

I just sat there speechless for a second, because I didn't actually know. I'd never thought about that before.

"Does she know what you did for her?" Posie asked. "Does she know it was you?"

"Everybody knew I drove the dean's Peugeot through the wall of the Beeswax Inn," I said. "That

17

wasn't exactly a big secret. But nobody knew why. At least not until last month, when Thorne called Sophie up and told her."

"Told her what?" Posie said.

"That I was trying to save her."

Posie smiled. "Good old Thorne," she said.

"He wanted to do me a favor," I said.

Posie nodded. "So what are you going to do about her?" she said. "Are you going to see her?"

"I don't know," I said.

"Yes, you do," said Posie, and the two of us just stared at each other, hard.

"You're right," I said finally. "I do."

And it struck me at that exact moment: *Posie and I are breaking up.*

"I think you should go home now," she said, and I could tell she was about to start crying again.

I reached down and put my shirt on, and then I tied my shoes. "Posie," I said. "You know I lov—"

"Shut up," she said. "Just go."

And I left her room and went outside and got on my bicycle and rode home. As I lay in bed last night, staring at the ceiling, all I could think was, *Maybe I just made the biggest mistake of my life.*

Dec. 10, 6:15 P.M.

Haven't felt like writing for a while. I guess I've been kind of depressed about the breakup with Posie. Depressed in general.

I'm sitting in the living room with MTV on in the background, and I'm just lying here pretending I'm doing something other than being a veg. Swim practice today was pretty brutal. Mr. Davis really wants us to beat Ely this Friday, but I can't see how it's ever going to happen. Mostly because we SUCK.

I've been trying this new dive, a back two-and-a-half somersault with a one-and-a-half twist, which is the dive Ely's star, Lamar Jameson, used last time. He's good, but he's not that graceful. The main thing he has is this huge physical strength. That means he can put more power into his dive, but as Mr. Davis says, that doesn't necessarily mean he can put any "poetry" into it. Mr. Davis is trying to get me to put more "poetry" in my dives, but I'm still not sure how to do this unless I go out on the board in a tutu. Actually, Mr. Davis seems to think I have a fair amount of "poetry" in my routine already. I don't know what that means, but whatever it is, he says I've got it.

A sort of cool thing happened with Wailer during practice. Actually, I have to admit that I can't keep disliking Wailer. He's not a bad guy, really. And of course we have something in common now. Wailer and I can both be classified as "Posie's ex-boyfriends." It's something I wish I didn't have in common with Wailer, but I do. Oh, well.

Wailer is trying this new dive, a double somersault with a one-and-a-half twist—which is way too hard for him, but he seemed determined to figure it out. Again and again he tried to do the dive, and every time he pretty much just fell off the end of the board like someone had shot him, and did a bellyflop. But the amazing thing was that he didn't get discouraged. He just kept getting out of the pool and trying it again and again. Finally, he sat down on the bench next to me.

"I think I'm getting the hang of it," he said, although he definitely wasn't.

And then he gave me this pathetic look like, *I'm never going to get the hang of it*, and I suddenly realized Wailer—Señor Bellyflop, Posie's ex-boyfriend, Mr. Cement Shoes—is asking me for *advice*.

I wanted to tell him exactly how I'd do the dive, but then I stopped myself, because if I did that he'd just get depressed and think, sure, it's easy for you. So instead I said, "It's a hard dive. It took me a long time to figure out how to do it."

Wailer thought about that and then he said, "Yeah? It did?"

"Oh, yeah, like three months maybe," I said. "I think the hardest thing for me was getting any height off the board." Which was Wailer's problem. He was basically falling straight into the pool like a dead weight without getting any spring from the board.

"Yeah, well, that's definitely a hard part about it," Wailer said.

"You know what I thought about when I first started doing it? I pretended I was like a little kid on a trampoline and I was trying to touch the sky with my hands, you know?" I stood up and stretched my arms up over my head like you're supposed to. Wailer nodded.

"Yeah, that's the secret of it all right," he said.

I got my swim cap and said, "Well, anyway,

that's great. It's cool that you're figuring it out."
And then I walked toward the board, but as I did I
saw Mr. Davis looking at me as if he'd heard everything I'd said, and he kind of nodded at me approv-
ingly. I had this weird thought like, *diving coach, I
could be a diving coach when I grow up.* It was the
first time I'd ever thought about having some kind
of job that I wouldn't hate after I get out of college,
and that sort of gave me this picture of my life
spreading out in front of me and I had this very
good feeling, like anything was possible.

Later, after I'd done a few routines, I sat back
down and watched Wailer practice his double somersault with a one-and-a-half twist. Wailer stretched
his arms up toward the ceiling and then fell like a
bag of stones into the pool. I can see why Mr. Davis
sometimes looks like he could use a drink or two.

After practice, my buddy Thorne was waiting for
me outside the natatorium, leaning against the
hood of his Beetle.

"Jonah, dude," he said, and raised one hand to
smack against mine. It feels good to be friends with
him again, especially after things were so weird for a
while, when he was going out with Posie. Actually,
Thorne and Wailer and I all have something in common now. I remember how out of it Thorne was when
Posie dumped him for me. Now I totally get how

Thorne felt. Of course, getting dumped doesn't really mean the same thing to Thorne as it does to me. I've still got Sophie, who I think might be the love of my life. But for Thorne, girls are like buses—there will always be another one in a few minutes.

"What's shaking?" he said. "I never see you around, man."

"Maybe that's because I'm in the friggin' eleventh grade, Thorne. You're living the senior lifestyle."

"Lifestyle, right. Like sending out a million college applications is a way of life."

"Did you get them all out?" I asked.

"Actually, I've got a whole new angle on the college thing."

"Yeah?" I said.

Thorne is definitely going to need an angle to get into college. His parents are like, totally broke. Plus, he's not exactly at the top of his class, so he's not going to get in anywhere remotely cool unless he comes up with some amazing scheme. Still, if anybody can hustle his way into college, it's Thorne. He's definitely had a lot of "angles" over the years, like starting his "Love Rendezvous Connection" dating service on the Internet, or borrowing my clamshell collar after I hurt my neck so girls would think he'd been hurt, or even wearing a pair of clear glasses so he could seduce this girl bookworm he had the hots for. Thorne is definitely the most resourceful guy I know.

"Yeah," Thorne said. "You know how like, Mr. Woodward put together like, this whole list of lame-o schools for me to apply to, like Cheesemore and Boring U? All these joke schools? Well, my mom meanwhile has this list like, Harvard, Yale, Connecticut Wesleyan, Ohio Wesleyan, Nebraska Wesleyan, et cetera. So it's like I've been going nutso because there's this one list Woody put together, and there's this other list Mommy put together, and the schools on Woody's list I don't want to go to, and the schools on Mommy's list I'll never get in to. Right? Okay, so I finally figured it out. The answer to all our problems. You ready, Jonahboy? Two words: business major."

"Business major?" I repeated.

"Definitely. Like, you can go to these schools and instead of majoring in like, Shakespeare or calculus or whatever, you can major in stuff like Making a Gazillion Clamolas. Which is something I'm actually interested in. And get this. All of my little ventures over the last couple years—like the Love Rendezvous Connection and the venture capital stuff—are exactly what they're looking for. All my little moneymaking hobbies will actually help me get into these schools. I'm serious, I've got it nailed! I'm gonna major in money!"

A second before, I'd been feeling sorry for him, thinking about how maybe he was never going to be able to pull off the college thing, and now I was thinking, *Well, maybe he has a shot*. The "ventures" he'd set up over the last year or two probably *would* impress some business school. About the only thing I couldn't see him talking about on his application was his weekend job on his father's fishing boat, the *Scrod*. But knowing Thorne, he'd have an angle on that, too, like he'd call himself an "oceanic studies consultant" or something.

"So where are you applying?" I said.

"Babson. Thomas. Vicksburg. And the University of Central Florida."

"UCF?" I said. "You want to go to UCF?"

"Well, not really," he said. "But they've got this special program in Internet business. *They* called *me*—can you believe it? I'm being *recruited*!"

"Hey, how 'bout that, Thorne? You might be in Orlando next year," I said. But I was doing worse than that. I was imagining Thorne going to college with Sophie. Going to football games together. Frat parties. No parents. Sex whenever you wanted. It made my palms sweat just thinking about it.

"So what happened to Cecily?" I asked. "You guys still tight?"

"Definitely. I'm tight with her. I'm tight with

25

Cilla. I'm tight with Elanor Brubaker," Thorne said.

"You're dating all of them?"

Thorne laughed. "Jonah, dude. You're the only person in the whole state who uses the word *dating*. You've got this whole retro thing going."

"Dating is retro?" I said.

"The whole monogamy thing. It's like you're going to go out with some chick and then like, give her your pledge pin or something. Go to the prom. Have triplets."

I couldn't believe him. "Cilla and Cecily and Elanor are okay then, about you dating all of them?" I said.

"Man, you think I sit around discussing the whole situation with them?" Thorne said. "Jesus, Jonahboy, what's up with you? You been drinkin' the Stupid Sauce?"

"So you're going out with all of them at once, and they don't know you're doing it, and you feel all fine about it?" I said, incredulous.

"Fine, of course I'm fine! It's awesome! It's like having cable, except instead of channels, I got girls," Thorne laughed.

I shook my head. I guess I'll never understand. "How's the old man?" I said, changing the subject. "How's the *Scrod*?"

"The *Scrod* sucks. I can't wait to ditch that

thing." He looked sad, at least to the extent that Thorne ever looks sad.

"My old man's gonna be screwed, though. He can't run the boat himself. He's going to have to fold unless he finds somebody to help him." Suddenly Thorne's face lit up like a flashlight. "Hey, Jonah man! You're going to be around next year! How'd you like to take my gig on the *Scrod*?"

"Me? Forget it. Thanks, but no thanks." I really didn't want to wake up at the crack of dawn on a Sunday morning and net and gut stinking fish. Delivering pizzas and videos for First Amendment is just fine with me.

"Think about it, man. It's a cash cow. Haulin' in sea anemones and selling them to the Japanese! You can make five hundred bucks a weekend, no kidding."

Judging from the way Thorne is always trying to raise more cash, I had a pretty good idea that I wouldn't be making anywhere near five hundred bucks a weekend—maybe more like fifty, *maybe*.

"You think I want to spend weekends floating around with your dad on the *Scrod*?" I said. "No thanks, Thorne. Really. I got a job."

"I'll tell him you're interested," Thorne said.

"I'm not!" I protested.

"Whatever, I'll just mention it."

"Don't."

"You're not committing yourself now," he assured me.

"No, I'm not committing myself now," I insisted. "I'm saying *no.*"

"You have an open mind," he said.

"I don't," I said.

"Good. Well, at least that's all settled. Now let me ask you something else. What are you going to do about Sophie?" Thorne said. "You gonna do her, or what? Posie says you guys have broken up for good."

I felt kind of mad at Posie for talking to Thorne about us. I guess I forget sometimes that Posie is as close to Thorne as she is to me, since the three of us have known each other practically since the womb. But I wasn't sure I wanted Posie's breakup with me to be something that she talked to Thorne about behind my back. I was still kind of sad about it.

"Yeah," was all I said.

"So are you going to see her? Sophie, I mean?" Thorne asked me.

"I don't know," I said. "We've been talking on the phone. She wants to get together over Christmas break, at Disney World."

"Disney World! You and Sophie! Awesome!" He was smiling like he was the one who was going to see her. "This is the best news I've heard all week."

"Please don't tell anyone. Okay? It's a secret."

"Hey, Jonah," Thorne said, flicking his fingers through his goatee. "If you can't trust *me*, who can you trust?"

I was about to laugh right in Thorne's face, but at that moment along came this incredible-looking girl I'd never seen before. She was like, six feet tall, skinny but not too skinny, with blond hair that fell below her waist. I'd never seen hair that long.

"Hey, Elanor! What's up!" Thorne wrapped his arms around her waist and tried to kiss her on the lips. She turned her head so his kiss landed on her cheek.

"This is Jonah Black," Thorne said.

She looked at me like she was looking at something through the wrong end of a telescope. I felt like I was shrinking.

"Jonah's in eleventh grade."
Thanks, Thorne.

"Hello," Elanor said, in a voice that suggested it might be nice if I fell through a trapdoor into a pit of flames.

"Elanor goes to St. Winnifred's," Thorne said.

St. Winnifred's is this unbelievably snooty girls' prep school in Lauderdale-by-the-Sea. It costs more to go there than it does to go to most colleges.

"Shall we?" Elanor said, and nodded toward the Beetle.

"We shall," said Thorne.

The two of them got into the car.

"Later, dude," Thorne called out the window to me.

"Later," I said, and went and got my bike. As I was undoing the chain I watched Thorne and Elanor drive away. Watching them take off made me feel sort of lonely. And stupid for not having my driver's license.

I went home and lay on my bed and listened to music for a while. Radiohead again. But that got way too depressing, so I went into the kitchen for some food. There was my sister, Honey, drinking Jolt cola. She looked up at me and blinked. There was another set of eyes on top of her eyelids. Temporary tattoos. I don't think anyone except Honey would have put them on their eyelids.

"That looks awesome, Honey," I said. "No wonder you're in the genius section at school."

"Hey," Honey said, and she blinked at me again. She was wearing a black T-shirt that had so many holes in it, it looked like it had been run over with a lawnmower. "Don't hate me because I'm beautiful," she said.

"That's not why I hate you," I said back.

I got a bag of Fritos and came back to my room and turned on my mother's radio show and wrote this.

Miss von Esse's class. Today we're reviewing the "subjunctive mood" in German class, which we did last month but apparently no one got it, because Miss von Esse is basically starting it all over from scratch. The subjunctive is this messed-up verb tense you use when you're discussing something that "might be." As opposed to something that "is." The story she's using to explain this is this bizarre thing called "Wenn die Haifische Menschen wären," which means, "If Sharks Were People." It's this whole description of what the world would be like if sharks could walk around and bite you.

Miss von Esse is wearing an off-white shirt without any sleeves and you can see her bra through it, which definitely makes class more interesting. The

31

top of the armholes are a little dark where she's been sweating. I wonder what Miss von Esse is sweating about. I wonder if she has a boyfriend or what her story is. Maybe she's just hot.

I delivered a video to her house once. I would love to sit around and watch movies with Miss von Esse. We could make some popcorn in the microwave, and while it's microwaving we melt butter in a little pot on the stove and she puts the popcorn in an orange bowl and pours the butter on top and then shakes garlic salt onto it and we watch *Return of the Jedi* and our fingers are touching in the popcorn bowl and then she puts her palm on top of mine and pushes it down into the bowl so our two hands are covered in greasy, steaming hot popcorn. Sophie turns to me with her big sad eyes and says, "Jonah Black, can you think of a good use of the subjunctive mood?"

And I say, "Uh . . ."

She frowns and scolds me. "Maybe you weren't paying attention," she says. Sophie is standing at the front of the classroom holding her chalk, and the sweat stains under her arms are bigger now. She turns and writes, "Wenn Jonah Black hören werde," which means, "if Jonah Black were listening."

I just stare at the words blankly, and everybody is looking at me like I'm some sort of freak.

Miss von Esse raised her arm to write on the board. Her armpit was shaved, not like last Friday when she had pretty bad armpit stubble. I guess she shaved her pits over the weekend. I can picture her standing in the shower with a pink disposable razor and her arm raised over her head. Now she wants to do her legs, but there's no comfortable way to prop her foot up so she can reach, so she sits down in the bath. And now that she's in there she decides to run a nice warm bubble bath with this violet bath gel that smells of grapes and fresh-cut grass. Sophie lies back in the bubble bath and closes her eyes. Her hair is piled on top of her head, and the bubbles come right up to her neck. She's listening to country-western music on the radio and it makes her laugh it's so hokey.

"Well?" she says.

I looked up to see Miss von Esse staring at me expectantly.

And Miss von Esse said, "If Jonah Black were paying attention . . . Please finish the sentence, Jonah."

I thought about it. "If I'd been paying attention," I said. "Um. We . . . we wouldn't be having this conversation?"

Fortunately, Miss von Esse laughed. And then she made me translate it into German.

After school today I was walking along the beach, just thinking about the situation I've gotten myself into. I knew where I was headed. The life-guard tower. And right after I got to the top of it, Pops Berman climbed up after me.

"Hey, Chipper," he said. He was out of breath.

"Hiya, Pops," I said. "How are you?"

"Not good," he wheezed.

"No? You been sick?"

"I'm always sick, Chipper. I got a liver like a piece a Swiss cheese." He shook his head. "Time's runnin' out."

"Swiss cheese?" I said.

"You got it, son. Eighty years of pepper vodka and this is how you wind up. You be smart, don't be like me, okay?"

"Okay," I laughed. "I won't drink pepper vodka for eighty years."

"And the ladies—you're walkin' the doggy with the ladies like I told you? While you're young and you still can?"

I shrugged.

Pops Berman covered his face with his hands. "Oh, no," he said. "Now what?"

34

"Well, you know my friend Posie? The girl I was seeing?"

"The surfboard mopsytop?" Pops said.

"Yeah, well, I was about to have sex with her the other night, and I did this stupid thing," I started to explain.

"You called her by the name of the other one. The one up North," Pops said, like it was the most obvious thing in the world.

I just stared at him. How could Pops know that? "How did you know?" I demanded.

He shrugged. "I'm psychic, I don't know. So your Posie hit the roof. Gave you what for. Am I right?"

"Yeah."

"And now you're sitting here kicking yourself. Thinking you're Kid Loser. You wanna plunge into the ocean blue wearin' lead pajamas," Pops said.

I didn't answer him.

"Well, don't you do it, Chipper," he told me. "There will be other chances to walk the doggy."

"Well, that's the thing. See, Sophie—that's the girl from Masthead—she's coming to Orlando in a couple of weeks," I explained. "She wants me to meet her at a hotel. In Disney World. She says she loves me."

Pops Berman smiled and slapped me on the back. "Hot dog!" he said. When I didn't smile back, his face changed. "Now what?" he said.

35

"I can't just run off and shack up with Sophie in some hotel!" I told him.

"Sure you can. You can do just about anything," Pops said.

"I can't. I don't have enough money for one thing," I said.

"How much do you need?" Pops said.

"To spend three days at a hotel? Eat? I don't know. But it's more than I have from delivering pizzas, I can tell you that."

Pops reached into his pocket and got out his wallet. "How's about three hundred bucks? You think that'll do it?" he said.

He held the bills out to me—three crisp new one-hundred-dollar bills. I must have looked like I'd been struck by lightning.

"Yeah, you're right," he said. "Better make it five."

He handed me five hundred dollars.

"I can't take your money, Pops!" I said.

"Why in hell not?"

"Five hundred dollars?"

"Listen Chipper, I got money lying around like moldy cheese," Pops said. "What am I going to spend five hundred bucks on? Vitamins?"

"I can't take your money," I insisted.

"Goddammit," he said. He held his cane up over one shoulder like he was going to strike me

with it. "Now you listen up, Chipper. I been watching you screw things up month after month now.
You got this one chance to make things right. You
go up to Disney World and shack up with that girl
and you take her out to a nice dinner and the two of
you ride around on Space Mountain and you walk
that little doggy of yours like he's never been
walked before. And when you get done, you come
back here and you tell me all about it. And if you
don't do exactly what I just told you to do, so help
me God I'm going to pound you so hard with this
cane you're going to look like succotash. Do you
understand me, Chipper, or don't you?"

I looked at him for a second. He looked like a
weird statue or something, or the figurehead from a
sailing ship. I nodded, and Pops sat down.

"Dammit, now you've given me palpitations," he
said, clutching his heart.

"Are you really okay, Pops? You're not going to
croak on me are you?" I joked, although I really *was*
worried.

"Hell, everybody's going to croak," he said.
"Better me than you."

"But I mean, you're not going to croak this second or anything?" I said.

"No, no," Pops said, and he reached over and
patted me on the back. "Not today."

"I guess I should say thank you," I said. "For the money and everything."

"I guess you should shut your clapper," Pops said, coughing so hard it sounded like his lungs were going to fly out of his mouth.

"Okay." I guess Pops doesn't like it when people say thank you.

"Now you listen to me, Chipper. I've been around a long time and I'm gonna drop dead one of these days, and between now and then I got just one job to do, and that's making sure you don't reach manhood a total idiot. Now you take that money and you find out what it's really like to love a woman, and to have her love you back. You learn that and maybe your life won't be completely worthless, and I can say *my* life wasn't a total waste."

Hearing him say that made me really sad. "You really think that? Your life was a waste?" I said.

"No, I didn't say that. It's not a waste yet," Pops said. "I still got you, Chipper. I'm betting it all on you."

I looked out at the ocean. The waves were choppy. A fierce breeze was blowing in from the Atlantic. I felt kind of strange, knowing that Pops was "betting it all on me." I don't know if I can handle the responsibility.

"Hey, Pops, what did you used to do before you retired?" I asked him.

"You mean a million years ago? When Grover Cleveland was President?" He laughed. "Fireman. Staten Island."

"Wow. You were a fireman? Cool!" I'd never met a real fireman before.

"Yeah, I guess. Half the buildings we saved we should have let burn to the ground. Bunch of eye-sores," Pops said.

"And were you married?" I said. "Is there a Mrs. Pops?"

Pops kept looking out at the ocean. His chest rose up and he heaved this huge, painful sigh.

"No, Chipper. There's no Mrs. Berman. There was going to be, but there wasn't." He looked at me, then dug his hand back into his pocket. He pulled out his wallet again and held it open. Inside was a picture of a beautiful young woman. It looked like it was taken in the 1940s.

"Wow," I said. "She's gorgeous."

"Rosemary Mahoney," he said. "Army nurse."

"Wow," I said again.

"Dead. Heart attack, age twenty-two. Can you believe that? Totally healthy young woman. Walking off the ferry with me one day, she put her hand on her heart and said, 'Oh, I feel tired.' Next thing you know, she falls over. Dead on the street. That was 1948."

"And you never—"

"Nah," he said. "Oh, lotsa times I thought about other girls. I mean I wanted to and all, Chipper. But it's kind of like when I was a kid and I had this dog and the dog died and my old man said, let's get another dog, and I said, no, dammit, I already had a dog."

Pops stood up. "Now look what you made me do. I'm sitting here thinking about the past!" He climbed down the ladder of the lifeguard tower and shook his cane at me. "You remember what I said. You show that girl a good time, and then you come back here and tell me all about it. Or else I'll smack ya."

I watched Pops Berman walk across the sand back toward Niagara Towers. Usually when he walks away from me he sings. But this time he didn't.

NORTHGIRL999: Hi Jonah!

JBLACK94710: Hi Northgirl. It's been a while since I've heard from you.

NORTHGIRL999: I've been away, actually.

JBLACK94710: Away? Where?

NORTHGIRL999: Never you mind. Are you okay? People say you're acting a little strange.

JBLACK94710: People? What people?

NORTHGIRL999: Never you mind.

JBLACK94710: You don't want me to know anything about you, do you?

NORTHGIRL999: Well, your not knowing who I am is like the only thing I have on you.

JBLACK94710: What do you mean?

NORTHGIRL999: I mean if you knew who I was you wouldn't talk to me.

JBLACK94710: Why wouldn't I talk to you?

NORTHGIRL999: You don't talk to me now. You don't think I'm important. I'm not even on your radar.

JBLACK94710: So you're somebody that I see all the time?

NORTHGIRL999: Yes.

JBLACK94710: You're not Pops Berman are you?

NORTHGIRL999: Who?

41

JBLACK94710: And please tell me you're not my sister Honey.

NORTHGIRL999: Hey, what's the deal with your sister Honey, anyway? She's a genius, right?

JBLACK94710: Yeah.

NORTHGIRL999: But how come she hangs out with all those losers? And walks around with her boobs practically falling out of her shirt. What's up with that?

JBLACK94710: I don't know. She says it's her personal style.

NORTHGIRL999: And she's going to Harvard?

JBLACK94710: Yeah, she got in early.

NORTHGIRL999: Whoa. She must be psyched.

JBLACK94710: I don't know. She acts all annoyed about it, like she had no choice because she's a genius and everyone expects her to go there.

NORTHGIRL999: Wait. Isn't she your little sister? How come she's going to college?

JBLACK94710: She skipped a grade. And I got held back. I told you that.

NORTHGIRL999: Sorry to rub it in.

JBLACK94710: Hey, you never answered my question.

NORTHGIRL999: Which question?

JBLACK94710: You're not Honey, are you?

NORTHGIRL999: Your sister? Yuck!

JBLACK94710: Never mind. You are a girl, though, right? You promise me this isn't like Mr. Davis or someone?

NORTHGIRL999: Hang on a second, let me check. BRB. Yeah, I'm definitely a girl. And I definitely am totally in love with you. You are so hot. And you don't even know it.

JBLACK94710: Why won't you tell me who you are?

NORTHGIRL999: I like the fact that you can't figure it out. It keeps you thinking about me. Which is more than you'd do if you knew who I was.

JBLACK94710: Well I gotta tell you, Northgirl. I like this a lot better than when you were pretending you were in Norway, or Sweden, or whatever it was.

NORTHGIRL999: I had you going then Jonah! :)

JBLACK94710: So who says I'm acting weird?

NORTHGIRL999: Never mind. But you are. You're all messed up aren't you?

JBLACK94710: Yeah. I guess. I broke up with Posie Hoff.

NORTHGIRL999: You didn't!

JBLACK94710: I did.

NORTHGIRL999: Jonah, are you totally stupid? Posie is like the perfect girl. After me, I mean.

JBLACK94710: Yeah, well, she broke up with me, actually.

NORTHGIRL999: Why?

JBLACK94710: Because she figured out how obsessed I am with that girl from my old boarding school.

NORTHGIRL999: Sophie?

JBLACK94710: Jesus, you know everything. Hey, this isn't Dr. LaRue, is it?

NORTHGIRL999: Who?

<u>JBLACK94710:</u> So I guess it's all true. I am kind of screwed up right now.

<u>NORTHGIRL999:</u> Are you ever going to get together with that Sophie girl?

<u>JBLACK94710:</u> Well, to tell you the truth, she has this plan for us to rent a hotel room in Orlando in a week or two.

<u>NORTHGIRL999:</u> Whoa. Hard core.

<u>JBLACK94710:</u> So should I do it?

<u>NORTHGIRL999:</u> I don't know. Do you love her?

<u>JBLACK94710:</u> I think so. But I don't really know her. She's kind of a mystery.

<u>NORTHGIRL999:</u> Hmm. What if spending a day in a hotel with her takes away all the mystery? Will you still love her then?

<u>JBLACK94710:</u> I'm not sure.

<u>NORTHGIRL999:</u> I wish I was her. Sophie. I can't believe you're going to spend a weekend in a hotel with her. It sounds like a dream. Like, sex, then room service, then cable, then Disney World. It's like that place in Pinocchio.

<u>JBLACK94710:</u> What place?

<u>NORTHGIRL999:</u> The one where all the boys turn into donkeys.

<u>JBLACK94710:</u> Oh yeah! Pleasure Island! Man, that scared me when I was a kid.

<u>NORTHGIRL999:</u> Oh I liked it. It was like, they had this big party and then they got to be donkeys. I never figured out what was the big deal, like being a donkey is so much worse than being a puppet?

<u>JBLACK94710:</u> LOL.

NORTHGIRL999: Goddammit Jonah talking to U always makes me horny!

JBLACK94710: You're feeling horny?

NORTHGIRL999: Jonah are you kidding U are so completely HOT. I just want to sit in this big bed hold U and kiss you until U laugh your head off.

JBLACK94710: Hey, do you look anything like those nude pix you sent me?

NORTHGIRL999: Wouldn't you like to know.

JBLACK94710: You're not going to tell me anything, are you?

NORTHGIRL999: Oh Jonah. Use your imagination.

JBLACK94710: I'm trying.

NORTHGIRL999: Uh oh. Gotta go. Talk to you later.

JBLACK94710: Wait. Come back. Don't go yet.

JBLACK94710: Northgirl? Hello?

Dec. 16

Well, my plans to meet up with Sophie are already blown. I failed my driving test today. Now I'm not sure how I'm going to get up to Orlando. Of course, even if I'd passed the test I'm not sure I'd have been able to negotiate Phase Two of my Not Very Top Secret Plan, which was to get Honey to loan me her Jeep. But I guess I don't have to worry about that now. What am I going to do? Ride my bike?

The funny thing is, it was sort of Sophie's fault I flunked my test. There I was, sitting behind the steering wheel of Mom's station wagon, waiting for the examiner to show up. Then the door swung open and this woman sat down in the passenger's seat and the first thing I thought was, whoa, she looks like she's practically my age. I was expecting some really old guy with a clipboard, but no, instead I got this amazing girl who couldn't have been more than eighteen, and she was wearing this little skirt with blue flowers on it and a white T-shirt. The badge pinned above her right breast was the only clue that she worked for the DMV.

I looked at the badge, which had her name on it, Ms. Teasdale, and I thought, *So what happened to her?* Did she drop out of high school and like, start working for the DMV? And how come? Like, was there some whole scandal like there was with me? I wondered if Ms. Teasdale was her name at all. I mean it's possible she'd put a fake name on the badge to keep guys from calling her at home. Not that that's what I was thinking about doing, but her hair was really shiny and she was definitely cute. I wondered what it would be like to call her up and say, "Hey, I'm that guy you gave the driving test to last week, maybe do you, like, want to go out sometime and I don't know, like, drive around?"

As I adjusted my seat and the mirrors and let out the parking brake, Ms. Teasdale was sketching on a sketch pad like Sophie used to do. She started to draw a tree. I remembered this place out in Valley Forge, like a half hour from Masthead, where there were these covered bridges and weeping willow trees and how cool it would have been to go out

47

there with Sophie and sit there by the creek, throwing in stones beneath the bridge and listening to the hollow, musical *ploop* sound they make as they hit the water while she sketched the willow trees on her pad.

So Sophie says to me, "Okay, would you put the car in drive, please, and pull out into traffic?"

I did what she asked and we headed up A1A toward Pompano Beach. I used the turn signal to change lanes and I was thinking, *I'm doing everything I'm supposed to.* I was THINKING ABOUT THE BIG PICTURE and DRIVING DEFENSIVELY and WATCHING OUT FOR THE OTHER GUY and LEAVING ONE CAR LENGTH BETWEEN MY VEHICLE AND THE ONE IN FRONT OF ME FOR EVERY TEN MILES PER HOUR I'M DRIVING and all that.

As I drive up A1A, Sophie puts her arm out the window like a little airplane wing, and raises and lowers it as we drive north. Then she pulls her hand back in and looks at her fingernails, which are jet black. Then she lowers the sun visor and pops up the vanity mirror and starts checking a contact lens. I'm trying to keep my eyes on the road, but it's a little distracting.

We cross the 14th Street bridge and Sophie says, "Go north on the Federal Highway."

I put on my blinker like a good boy and drive up

Route 1 past the Pompano Square Mall. We drive on without talking, but it's not a weird silence; it's totally comfortable, like the two of us understand each other and don't have to say a thing.

"You're doing very well, Jonah," she says at last.

"Really?" I say. "You think so?"

"Definitely," Sophie says. We drive around some more and just as we're passing Sea Ranch Lakes she starts fishing around in her purse for a Kleenex, and it looks like she's crying and I'm like, damn. So I turn down a residential street without any traffic and park next to this pier and I say, "Are you okay, Sophie?"

And she says, "No, I'm not okay."

"Do I know the reason?" I say.

And she says, "I think you do, Jonah. I just don't know what to say to you. It's like, you got yourself thrown out of school for me, and you never told anyone about me and Sullivan. You basically sacrificed yourself for me, just because you're a good guy. I don't know how to thank you, Jonah. I'm totally in your debt. I only wish I could think of some way to make you happy."

And I'm like, "You're making me happy just sitting there talking to me."

Sophie suddenly reaches forward and gives me this big hug, and I hug her back, and I can feel the back of Sophie's bra through her white T-shirt and her blond hair brushes my cheek and she lifts up her head and kisses me and she makes this little seagull sound. A little cry. I close my eyes and just feel our lips together, brushing softly against each other, and all of a sudden there was a terrible crashing sound and I was thrown against the wheel and all the red lights in the dashboard started flashing.

The guy I hit got out of his car. It was a Lincoln Continental. Ms. Teasdale turned to me and said in this angry, disappointed voice, "You stay in the car, Mr. Black."

I sat there for a long time just thinking, STUPID STUPID STUPID. Finally, Ms. Teasdale got back in the car and said, "Please return to the DMV." Fortunately, Mom's car is fine, although the Lincoln's bumper was kind of dented.

"I guess this means I didn't pass my test, huh?" I said, stating the obvious.

And Sophie looks at me sadly and says, "I guess not."

AMERICA ONLINE MAIL
12-16, 9:43 P.M.

To: JBlack94710@aol.com
From: BetsD8@MastheadAcademy.edu

Hey Jonah, it's Betsy Donnelly, remember me? I know you do. I feel bad about not writing you since you left Masthead, but whatever. It was weird because I was thinking about you today, like about what you did for Sophie O'Brien and everything. All of the girls here at Masthead are so grateful to you, and if you ever came back up here to visit you'd find out you are like, a total hero. I don't know if you heard that Sullivan didn't come back to school this fall. He's at Valley Forge Military Academy, which serves him right, if you ask me. I saw him in downtown Wayne last weekend in Harrison's, and he was wearing this stupid little uniform and he had his head shaved practically bald and I thought, way to go Jonah!

Anyway, I talked to Sophie a little bit today and she was being all weird like she usually is and she told me she had been talking with you on the phone and was going to go down to Florida to see you over break. That sounds incredibly romantic and everything. You must be psyched.

But I just wanted to say this one thing and maybe my writing this to you out of nowhere is really off base, but I think Sophie is a really bizarre girl. I get a very strange vibe from her. I can't explain it, so maybe it's stupid to be writing this.

--- ■ ---

But if you do meet up with her, watch out. Because there is definitely something sketchy about her and I don't want you to get hurt. I think you've been hurt enough already over her.

So that's what I think, and if this was the wrong thing to say, I'm sorry but I thought you'd want to know.

You can call me anytime if you want to talk about this. I'm staying here over Xmas break—it's just me and two other girls in the girls' dorm—so I'd be glad to talk to somebody. Or whatever!

Love,
Bets

Dec. 17, 4:21 P.M.

Well, the big meet with Ely is tomorrow, and I have to say I'm psyched, even though I already know we're going to lose. I know I'm going to do fine, but the rest of the team is *so* lame. I know that sounds terrible to put in writing, but it's true.

I have to say I'm also feeling a little weird about that e-mail I got from Betsy Donnelly. I mean it was great to hear from Betsy. It's the first time anybody from Masthead has written me at all since I got thrown out.

But her letter made me mad at first, like who is Betsy Donnelly to come out of nowhere and say, *Watch out*? I guess I sort of get the same kind of feeling from Sophie, though. There's definitely something weird about her. But it's the something weird that I think I'm in love with. What's wrong with that?

When I got back from school today no one was home, so I dialed up the Porpoise in Orlando and I booked a room. I don't know how I'm getting there, but I'm definitely going. They asked me what kind of bed I wanted and I said king size, and the woman said, "for just one person?" and I said, "Yes." I love big beds. I remember when I was a kid and Mom and Dad still lived together they had a king size. Honey and I used to jump up and down on it like it was a trampoline. I guess Dad probably still has the same bed. It's pretty creepy to think of him and Tiffany sleeping on it when he and Mom used to sleep on it, too.

So then I decided I should call Sophie and tell her I'm going to be there and to make a final plan. The only way to contact her is by ringing the dorm phone, and I could just picture that phone while it was ringing—the one phone at the end of the hallway. Finally, someone picked it up and I asked for Sophie and the girl who answered said, "Just a sec." I heard the girl's steps going down the dorm hallway and I could see exactly what it looked like—the black-and-tan tiled floor and the fluorescent lights and the smell in the hallway like someone needs to do her laundry.

I listened to all these sounds coming over the phone and all I could think was, *In a minute Sophie's going to pick up.*

I heard the voice of the girl who'd answered the phone talking to someone and saying, "It's a guy," and then these other steps coming down the hallway and I thought, *It's her.*

And then Sophie picked up the phone and said, "Hello?" and her voice was like getting into bed after a long night out.

"It's me," I said.

And she said, "Who?"

And I said, "Jonah. Jonah Black?"

And with this sudden rush of enthusiasm she says, "Oh, Jo-nah! How *are* you?"

"I'm good," I said.

"What's up?" she said.

"Well, I wanted you to know I booked a room. At the Porpoise. For the twenty-seventh and the twenty-eighth. I still haven't figured out what I'm going to tell my mom. Or how I'm getting there. But I did it."

There was this long pause, and for a second I thought, *Oh, no, she's upset, she never thought I'd do it.*

But then she said, "Oh, that's so great, Jonah. I can't believe we're going to spend some time together!"

"I know," I said. I couldn't believe it, either.

"Well, we're getting there the night of the twenty-sixth, I think. So the next day I'll find out what room you're in and I'll call you, okay?" she said.

"You'll call the room?" I said. My voice sounded a little shaky.

"Yeah. What time are you getting in on the twenty-seventh?" she asked.

"I don't know yet. I haven't figured out how I'm getting there. That's the next thing I have to work on. But I'll aim for early afternoon, like one or two?" I said.

"Okay. Why don't I call you at like, two-thirty then, all right? Does that sound good?" she said.

"Yes," I said. It sounded great.

"I can't wait to see you. I think about you all the time," she said.

"I think about you, too, Sophie. I got a king-size bed in my room." The minute I said it I thought, *stupid*! I sounded like the lamest idiot in the universe.

"That'll be nice," Sophie said, and she didn't sound like she thought I was stupid. "I can't wait to lie around with you."

Oh, my God, I thought I was going to turn into a pile of sand hearing her say that. Then she said, "Of course I want to go to Disney World, too. Have you ever been there, Jonah?"

I *have* been there, but not since I was about ten. "Oh, sure," I said. "I can show you around."

"I'd like that," Sophie said. Then there was this long pause and I could hear the sound of her breathing, like the actual sound of her breath against the receiver. "I still can't believe you're real," she said finally, in this kind of dreamy voice.

"I'm real," I said. "Are you real?"

"I don't know," she said, in this kind of quavery voice. "I'm definitely trying."

I thought about the e-mail Betsy had sent me and I really wanted to ask her, *So Sophie. What's the deal with you, anyway?* But I couldn't figure out how to ask it without sounding rude.

Then there was the sound of lots of voices coming down the hallway. Some of them were guys. "Hang on a second," Sophie said. Everything got all muffled but I could sort of hear Sophie's voice, talking to these other people. Then she took her hand off the receiver and I heard people laughing in the background and Sophie was laughing, too.

"Hello?" I said.

"Sorry," Sophie said into the phone.

"Who was that?" I asked.

"Oh, you know. Just the usual Masthead morons," she said.

"I know all about them," I said. And then someone

57

—— ∎ ——

in the background shouted something down the hallway, and Sophie shouted back, "Shut up!"

"I can't believe I'm going to get to see you," she
said again.

"Me neither," I said.

"Well anyway. I kind of have to go now. So I'll
see you on the twenty-seventh, Jonah. I can't wait."

I said I couldn't wait, either, and then Sophie
said, "Bye-bye," and the line went dead. I sat there
in my room listening to the dead sound for a while,
then I hung up, too.

(Still Dec. 17, 11:31 P.M.)

Now I've lied to Mom. I waited for her to come
back from her radio show, and I told her I had an
interview at UCF on the twenty-seventh. I said that
Thorne was interviewing there and I thought maybe
I'd get a head start on looking at colleges, see what
it's like. I haven't actually asked Thorne yet, but I
know he wants to check out UCF sometime, so why
not on the twenty-seventh?

Mom was in one of her emotional moods. She
hugged me and started to cry, and I said, "Mom,
why are you crying?"

"Because I'm so happy for you. My little Jonah's

all grown up!" she said. She wiped her eyes with a paper towel.

"I'm not all grown up," I said. "Besides, I'm still a junior—" I started to say, but then her cell phone went off.

"Bup, bup, bup," she said, holding up her hand to quiet me. "I have to take this." She went into her bedroom and closed the door. I could tell it was Mr. Bond calling, because she started cooing as soon as she closed her door.

I think it's depressing how easy it is to lie to your parents. When I was a little kid, I remember Dad saying, "If you ever lie, I'll know." I'm not sure how I thought he'd know, but it sounded pretty scary, like he had some kind of gland that would kick in if I ever lied to him. So I didn't, and I lived for years with the fear of him knowing if I ever lied. It was years later that I figured that out that when Dad said he could tell when I was lying, *he* was lying. It turned out he didn't have the slightest idea what the difference was between what was real and what was made up.

I remember this one time I was about seven and Honey was six, and we'd had this dog named Toby who died, and Dad had told me that the dog was buried on this farm owned by Dr. Boyers, the vet. Now that I think about it, Toby had probably been cremated at Dr. Boyers's and disposed of there. But Dad made it sound like there was this actual tombstone that said TOBY on it somewhere on Dr. Boyers's farm. So one day me and Honey went over there looking for it. Dr. Boyers lived on this big old farm and it was all pretty run-down, and we kind of got lost on the property, just stumbling around looking for Toby's tombstone, which we figured had to be pretty big since Toby was a St. Bernard.

Anyway, along came Dr. Boyers, who I now think was probably a lesbian only back then I didn't know what that was, and she stopped Honey and me and asked us what "we kids" thought we were doing on her property, and we said we were looking for Toby's gravestone because we heard he was buried there. But Dr. Boyers laughed and said, "You kids better get your story straight. That's the worst lie I've ever heard." And she threw us off her property and yelled at us for trespassing.

And I remember that being this whole big insight because when you're a kid you think the one thing you can fall back on, when everything else fails, is to tell the truth. But this time we'd told the truth, and this adult had assumed it was a lie anyway. Like, telling the truth had made absolutely no difference. It was an awful thing to learn. It was like one of the fundamental laws of the universe changing, and there suddenly not being any gravity. From then on I had to live in a world where telling the truth didn't necessarily save you from anything.

—— ■ ——

Dec. 18, 11:53 P.M.

The first reason I knew the swim meet was going to be weird was that Wailer—Señor Bellyflop—pulled off the double somersault with a one-and-a-half twist. I mean it was perfect.

The crowd, including Honey and Thorne and Posie, went crazy, but not nearly as crazy as they should have. I actually felt really proud of Wailer. He had worked and worked on this dive, and the one time in his whole diving career he actually did it right was when it mattered.

He got out of the water with this big grin on his face and everybody on the bench gave him high-fives and congratulated him. Mr. Davis just looked at him and said something like, "You're full of surprises, aren't you son?" Then the scores came up, and they were good. Mr. Davis was psyched—we all were. Then the coach looked over at me and nodded, like he was saying, *You helped him learn this, Jonah. Good work.* It was kind of exciting. But when I looked over at Wailer, he was looking up at Posie in the stands. She wasn't looking at him—she was busy talking to Thorne—but it struck me that Wailer was still trying to impress her. Maybe even more now that Posie and I had broken up, and she was available.

As I looked up in the stands I saw that Watches Boys Dive was sitting behind Posie and Thorne. She's that girl who always comes to swim practice and sits in the bleachers. That's not really her name. I don't know who she is, but she looks Indian. She saw me looking at her and she suddenly smiled this huge ear-to-ear smile, and then she waved her fingers kind of shyly at me. And I was like, whoa, cool.

The diver from Ely got up, this guy everyone calls "Fats" Cleveland. He's always fun to watch because he's this huge guy, not the normal build for a diver at all. He usually does these relatively simple dives, but he has amazing control for a guy who's like, the size of a bus. He did the same dive as Wailer, which was a surprise because I'd never seen him do anything that challenging. Also, doing the somersaults was especially hard for him because it's not easy to flip that much weight around, especially if you don't have the body strength. Still, for all that I have to admit that it was kind of cool to watch him; there was something beautiful about a huge fat kid twisting around in space. Fats's dive really wasn't all that technically proficient, but the novelty of him was enough to melt the hearts of a couple of the judges, and his scores reflected that. That kind of pissed me off. I mean, I'm all for people trying to stretch themselves, but it's not like I think you should give somebody a 9.1 on a 4.5 dive just because they're really huge.

Anyway, Martino Suarez did his usual back flip, and the next guy up on Ely's team did the same dive, only a little better, and the crowd went crazy. It was definitely exciting. I like diving against a team as good as Ely because it makes you push yourself a little bit farther. It's worth saying that about ninety-five percent of the Ely fans were black, and about seventy-five percent of Don Shula High fans were white. That's another thing I like about sports—everybody kind of comes together. Anyway, the meet was intense. It was so incredibly close.

Our guys did better than anyone expected, and Ely had a couple of mishaps. After that first outing, the judges started taking points off for Fats's technique. By the time it was down to the last two divers, me and Lamar Jameson, the meet was tied.

Lamar climbed up the high dive. He's so damn huge. It's like even his *ears* are muscular. He walked to the end of the board and looked right at me with this big grin on his face. Then he turned around and balanced on the end of the board with just the balls of his feet and his toes touching, and the rest of his feet sticking out into empty space.

Everybody got really quiet. He held his arms out to his sides like a bird and it was just beautiful to watch. Lamar is always good, but I'd never seen him work the crowd like this before. I mean everybody wanted him to do well, even the people on our side. He pressed down with his legs and the board sprang up. Airborne, he reached up high to the ceiling and twisted his body in a full turn; then he tucked his arms and head in and spun over, once, twice, two-and-a-half times before straightening his arms and sailing down like an arrow, slicing perfectly into the water.

Everyone went crazy. 9.1/9.2/9.0/9.1/9.2.

Now it was my turn. The creepy thing was that Lamar and I had both signed up to do the exact same dive. And as I climbed up the ladder, I thought, *I wonder if Lamar knew I'd do exactly this,*

———— ■ ————

*and so he signed up for a dive he didn't think I
could do as well as him.*

Not that I can't do a two and a half somersault
with a full turn starting from the inverse position,
but it is not my favorite dive. It definitely screws
with your brain. Especially the way you have to start
out with your back to the pool, balancing on your
toes at the edge of the board. I'm not crazy about
that, but it's just one more thing you have to psych
yourself up to do.

So there I was, standing at the end of the board
with about half of my body hanging out into empty
space. I tried to totally shut down all thoughts and
just concentrate on the dive.

But I couldn't concentrate. Instead I thought
about the last couple of meets when, at the critical
moment, all I could think about was Sophie. And of
course it started to happen again.

I thought about Sophie and me in the hotel in
Orlando, and what she looks like with her clothes
off. She has this fine, fine blond hair on her arms
and it makes her skin feel so soft, and I kiss her
right in the crook of her elbow and her skin tastes
the way daisies smell.

I heard the crowd start to murmur behind me and
I realized I'd been standing at the end of the board
for a long time and that I'd lost my concentration.

There was no way I could do the dive unless my mind was totally clear, and suddenly I felt really afraid, like I'd forgotten how to dive and what was I doing there anyway? I was sure I was going to screw everything up. So I tried to let everything drain out of me.

I raised my arms out to the side and then I felt my arms closing around Sophie's naked back and it is so smooth and soft and I can feel her breasts against my chest and her hair falling over my shoulder and her lips on my neck, kissing me softly and I'm wondering, *Are you thinking about me at this exact same second, Sophie, up there in Pennsylvania? Are people looking at you, wondering why you aren't leaping into the air like you're supposed to?*

Then I thought, *Come on, Jonah, do it. DO IT.*

So I pressed down on the board and sprang toward the ceiling and I did the dive like it was right out of a book. It was picture-perfect.

I wish Sophie had seen me do that dive. If she saw how well I can dive she might fall in love with me even more.

I heard the crowd roaring even while I was below the surface. I love hearing that muffled cheering getting louder and louder as I rise up. I got out of the pool and I looked at Lamar Jameson, who was sitting on the bench looking very serious, and then all of a sudden he cracked this huge smile and pointed at me and shook his head, like he was saying, *You're good, you bastard.*

9.1/9.3/9.0/9.1/9.2.

I'd beaten him by one tenth of a point. Everybody went nuts. We'd won the meet. The place went crazy. It was like the end of the Second World War when sailors were grabbing girls they didn't know and kissing them. The Ely guys were totally bummed. They just sat there on the bench with their faces in their hands—everybody except Lamar. I think he knew he was great, but just this one time I'd out-psyched him. Still, he knew we'd meet again and that he'd get me sooner or later.

I think he also knew how close I'd come to screwing it up again.

Our teams filed past each other shaking hands. Lamar and I were the last guys in line. He squeezed my hand hard, then gave me this weird look.

"Okay," he said to me. "You're good."

"Okay," I said back. "You, too."

Then we all headed out to the locker room. I looked up in the stands to see what Watches Boys Dive was doing, but she wasn't there anymore. Neither was Posie.

So here I am in history class, and we're stuck in the series of presidents after the Civil War, all of whom were basically winos or something: Rutherford B. Hayes, Garfield, Arthur, Cleveland, Harrison, Cleveland again—as if once weren't enough. And what's with the whole Chester Alan Arthur thing? I mean, like there was actually a President Arthur???? Seriously, who do they think they're kidding?

I wonder if some day the time we're living in right now will look like that to somebody. Like, they'll look back and go, Ford, Carter, Reagan, Bush, Clinton, Bush Junior, and they'll go: *Who?*

There is this girl behind me named Lauren Spellman and she has perfect knees. They are totally tanned and it's a real tan, too, not a fake one from some tanning cream. I want to tell her, *Listen, you better use sunscreen, it's not good for you being out in the sun all the time.*

And she says, "Oh, Jonah, you are so thoughtful. I mean, I have been with a lot of guys before, but nobody ever worried about me getting cancer before."

And I say, "Well, Sophie, you should take care of yourself."

And she says, "I try to, but it's hard."

I touch her arm and the hairs on it are as soft as moss in a forest, and the sunlight has warmed her skin. She reaches forward and puts her hand on the side of my face, and I can feel each finger on my cheek.

Now it's on to the Spanish-American War, I guess, and Mr. Bond is telling us about people saying *Remember the* Maine, which is the state that Sophie comes from. And I'm like, *Remember it? As if I could forget.*

(Still Dec. 19, later)

I'm in the cafeteria and guess what I'm eating for lunch again? Here at good old Don Shula High, every day is pizza day. They have pizza stix, those bread sticks you dip in a little bowl of sauce, and pizza rounds, which are like bagel pizzas. Sometimes it's plain pizza slices, and other days it's pepperoni. I mean I like pizza. It's one of my favorite foods. But between pretty much eating pizza every day at school, and then delivering pizzas for First Amendment after school, enough is enough already.

It's funny how all the girls have salad for lunch. I don't think I've ever seen a girl eat pizza. They put salad on their plates, and either eat it dry (which is about the grossest thing I can think of), or else they put the dressing on the side, or else they use the fat-free vinaigrette and maybe splurge for a yogurt. I think it's sad that girls don't allow themselves to enjoy food. There are a couple of girls in my class, like Tina Cleveland, who can't weigh more than ninety-five pounds. She never eats anything except dry lettuce, and after class she's in the gym on the treadmill, running it off.

They say that girls who are anorexic can't see themselves—like they look in the mirror and all they see is some huge person. It's really sad, but I think I can kind of understand what that's like. Seeing yourself as you really are is hard to do. Like, what do people think of me really? Do they see some athlete, because I'm good at diving? Do they see someone who thinks he's above it all, since I'm really a senior stuck in eleventh grade? Or do they see a loser who got thrown out of school in Pennsylvania and had to come home to Pompano Beach and repeat junior year? Can they tell I'm a virgin from the way I eat my pizza? Who knows.

(Still Dec. 19, 4:40 P.M.)

So Thorne was leaning against his Volkswagen Beetle as I came out of swim practice—the last one before break. He smiled when I saw him and said, "Jonah, dude. How's it hanging?"

"Fine," I said.

"So what's it like being the school hero?" he asked me.

"I'm not any hero," I said.

"Get out, dude! Winning that meet? You're like the golden boy. Man, if I were you I'd be cashing in!"

"Who says I'm not cashing in?" I said.

Thorne just smiled. "So what do you want to do? You want to drive around?"

I said okay and we took off in the Beetle. Thorne started driving south on A1A and we just looked out at all the expensive hotels and the ocean crashing on the beach.

"So I heard you failed your driving test," Thorne said.

I couldn't believe he knew! I hadn't told anybody

I was even taking it! How come Thorne always knows everything?

"Thorne, how did you find that out? Seriously," I said.

"Dominique told me."

"Dominique?" There is nobody at Don Shula named Dominique.

"Dominique Teasdale? Your driving examiner?" he said.

I remembered Ms. Teasdale, her shiny brown hair, and how upset she was when I ran the car into the back of that guy's Lincoln. Thorne had told me he'd met some new girl, but he didn't tell me who. I can't believe him sometimes.

"How are you planning on getting up to Orlando?" he asked. "So you and Sophie can have your little Disney hotel orgy?"

"I don't know," I said. "Now that I've flunked my test, it's kind of a problem. I don't have an alternate plan."

"Well, I have a plan for you, Jonah," Thorne said. "How about I drive you?"

"Really?" I acted all surprised, even though I'd been planning to ask him anyway. Either that, or steal Mom's car and drive it illegally, which was a pretty dumb idea. Although the whole plan to meet Sophie in Disney World was pretty crazy anyway.

"You don't mind?" I said.

"Why not, man? I was thinking I'd go up to UCF anyway, look around, maybe get an interview or something," he said. "Anyway, consider this my gift to you, Jonah. Think of me as your own Mr. Cupid Dude."

I looked at Thorne, with his shaggy hair and his goatee and his big-ass grin. He does sort of look like a Mr. Cupid Dude.

"That's awesome, Thorne. Thanks," I said.

"Nada," he said. "It'll be fun. A road trip!" He screeched the Beetle around a corner. "I gotta meet this Sophie chick, anyway. She sounds tasty."

Suddenly I felt kind of dizzy. I didn't want Thorne to meet Sophie. It would ruin everything.

"You want to meet her?" I said.

"Hell, yes," he said. "You got a problem with that?"

Actually, I did have a problem with it, but if he was giving me a ride I wasn't sure I could deny him a chance to at least meet her. Still, it made me uncomfortable. Sophie was from a whole different world, a whole different part of my life. I don't want those two worlds to meet. And even though he's my best buddy, I don't want Thorne's grubby paws anywhere near Sophie.

"So. Have you seen Posie?" Thorne said. "I hear she's already got a new boyfriend."

"What?" I said, stunned. I couldn't believe

Posie would start seeing somebody else so quickly. I guess I kind of figured she'd be all broken up about me and she wouldn't feel like dating anybody.

"Yeah. Since she ditched you, she's never home anymore. Everybody says she's got some new guy, but nobody knows who." Thorne glanced at me suspiciously. "You sure it's not you?"

"Me?" I said.

"It'd be just like the two of you to break up and then get back together and not tell anybody." He looked over at me. "But I guess you're on to bigger things."

"Yeah. I guess," I said, but thinking about Posie like that made me feel sad.

Thorne honked his horn at some girl I'd never seen before, and instead of giving him the finger, she smiled and blew him a kiss.

"You're a lucky man, Jonah," he said. "A girl like Sophie waiting for you in a hotel room. Damn, sometimes I wish I was you. Jonah Black, Teenage Stud!"

"Yeah, I'm definitely lucky," I said. But for some reason, I didn't feel all that lucky.

(Still Dec. 19, even later)

At five P.M. I headed over for my appointment with Dr. LaRue. As usual, I sat there looking at him with his itchy sweater and his short bristly mustache and his huge bald head. He looked like the full moon rising over a cornfield. Or something. Anyway, he asked me what was going on in my life and for some reason I started talking about Dr. Boyers and Toby and Honey and that time we went looking for the dog.

So I thought we were going to have this whole big discussion about telling the truth and lying.

But instead, he just asked me, "Do you love your sister, Jonah?"

"Of course I do," I said.

"Do you ever tell her?"

"Of course not," I said.

"Why not?"

"Because," I said, "if I did she'd punch me in the nose."

And Dr. LaRue laughed! It was like, the funniest thing he'd ever heard. He had to take his glasses off and wipe his face with a Kleenex.

That's when I realized I'd never made him laugh before. I guess we're making progress.

Saturday. I spent all day delivering pizzas and videos on my bike for Mr. Swede at First Amendment Pizza and the whole time I was thinking, *You know, I must be stupid to have a part-time job that pays as lousy as this.* I mean, I'm making like, six bucks an hour plus tips, which I don't even think is minimum wage. And I have to admit that for about three seconds I wondered how much money I could make working for Thorne's dad on the *Scrod*.

■

Dec. 21, 3:30 P.M.

I was going to do some Xmas shopping today but
Honey took her Jeep and Mom took the Audi so I
couldn't get a ride to the mall, and I don't feel like
riding my bike with a whole bunch of bags and stuff.
I hate shopping anyway. I never know what to get
people. It's like some object or something is supposed to symbolize how I feel about the people in
my family—and there's no way anything I could buy
in the Coral Springs Mall is going to sum that up.

I heard Honey come home around two-thirty.
She went into her room and threw some bags on the
floor and then the next thing I know she's standing
in my doorway with this look.

"What?" I said.

"You're up to something," she said.

"What am I up to?"

"That's what I can't figure out. But you're definitely scheming. You wanna let me in on the caper, Melon Butt?" she asked me.

"I don't have any caper," I insisted.

"Okay, fine, forget it. If you're going to keep it a government secret then fine," she said.

"I don't have a secret!"

"Of course you have a secret. Don't act like I'm an idiot."

"Right, you're going to Harvard, I forgot," I said. It was about the only thing I could think of that I knew would really bug her.

"Oh, eat me. You know I'm just trying to help you," Honey said.

"Help me? What do you want to help me with?" I asked her.

"Nothing. Forget it. You're hopeless," she said, disgusted. "I only want to say one thing. When you finish doing whatever stupid thing it is you're planning, and you're feeling like a total moron because you screwed it up, whatever it is, just remember that I came to you and asked if I could help you and you said, 'No, thank you, I prefer to be a total loser.' Okay?"

She started to go back to her room, but I said, "Honey?"

And she goes, "What?"

"Haven't you ever had a secret?" I said.

"Well, of course I have," Honey said. "But we're not talking about me."

"Well, maybe I want to have some secrets of my own," I told her. "Just because I don't want to share everything with you doesn't mean I don't love you."

"Oh, my God," she said, clutching her stomach. "Get me the ipecac syrup. I think I'm tastin' vomit chunks!"

"Never mind," I said.

"Listen, Fishbreath," she said. "This isn't about our widdle wuv that we share because we're brudduh and sistah! It's about you getting into some moronic jam. Ending up in jail. Getting thrown out of school, or something. I can't *wait* to find out what you're up to this time."

"How do you know I'm going to wind up in jail?" I protested. That might have been possible if I had to steal Mom's car. But that won't be necessary now that Thorne is driving me.

"Jesus, kid, how blind do you think I am? I know this has something to do with this supposed college trip you're taking on the twenty-seventh. I mean, that much is obvious. Like you'd ever go to UCF—I mean really! As if you'd ever go anywhere that doesn't have a diving team. So you're probably going somewhere other than Orlando. But where? And how will you get there? You can't drive. And what about money? You only have a hundred and thirty-eight dollars and fifty-seven cents in your checking account. You'll need more than that to pull off anything major. So I don't know, Monkey Nuts. I can't quite figure this out."

"How do you know how much money I have in my checking account?" I said, alarmed.

"Gee, I don't know, Lameness, maybe I'm Sherlock Holmes or something," she said.

"I don't like being spied on," I told her.

"Well, I don't like watching you walk into a pit of snakes with your pants down. But fine. Play it your way," Honey said.

She left the room, then came back a second later.

"You know what I think? I think you're going to Maine to see that chick from Masthead," she said. "Soapy."

"Sophie," I corrected her.

Honey looked at me as I said her name.

"Mmm-hmm," Honey said. "I get it."

"What do you get?" I said.

"Can I just say one thing? Take some long underwear. It's cold in Maine," Honey advised.

"Okay," I said. "If I go to Maine I'll take some long underwear. And when I'm all snug and warm

I'll say, *Thank you, Honey, for caring enough to make me toasty."*

"Fine," she said, and left. As she went down the hall she called out, "Remind me to leave you alone from now on."

"Wait," I yelled after her. I heard her door open, but she didn't go into her room.

"What?" she called back. She sounded annoyed, but still interested.

"Hey. When we were little kids. Do you remember the time we went looking for the place where Toby was buried?" I said.

Honey was quiet for a second. Then she called back, "Yeah. I remember that. There was this whole little graveyard. We put flowers on his grave."

"What? No we didn't," I said. "We got yelled at by Dr. Boyers. She didn't believe us when we told her what we were doing."

"Dr. Boyers?" Honey said. "Dr. Boyers wasn't there. It was Dr. Moynihan. I remember picking violets with his daughter, Megan. We put violets on Toby's grave and sang church songs."

"No, we didn't," I insisted. "We got yelled at. She chased us off the farm."

There was a long silence. Honey was standing in her doorway. "I remember picking violets," she said at last, then closed her door.

Today this kind of sad thing happened. School is out for break, so I got Mom to take me to the Coral Springs Mall. We got there by ten A.M. and agreed to meet back at the car at two-thirty P.M., which gave me enough time to shop for presents and maybe get some lunch. I did my Christmas shopping pretty quickly, because I really hate to shop. It always makes me feel like I'm incredibly retarded or something, like I don't speak the language of shopping. I want to get good presents for people, something that will show I put a lot of thought into it. But I can never find anything good. I got Mom a kind of silky robe, and I got Honey the new PJ Harvey CD. Good enough, I guess, but not great.

Then I went to the bookstore and bought Dad a

book. I can't even remember which one exactly except that I knew he'd like it because it has a submarine on the cover. I know I'm going to get a card from him soon with a check in it as a present. It always pisses me off that he can't be bothered to get me something personal. Although the money is good, especially now that I'm going to Disney World.

Anyway, with Mom, Dad, and Honey out of the way, I was all done with shopping, except that I wanted to buy something for Sophie. So I went into this shop called Afterthoughts that has earrings and stuff. I picked out a bunch of earrings and tried to imagine them in Sophie's ears. Finally I got her these cool ones by somebody named Holly Yashi. They're kind of hard to describe—kind of turquoise with these Asian-looking characters on them. I think she'll like them because I remember her having ones like this at Masthead.

I had them gift wrap the earrings, and then I started feeling pretty good because I realized I'm seeing Sophie in a few days, and it actually looks like it's really going to happen. I'm pretty excited.

Anyway, I had just left Afterthoughts when I suddenly saw Posie walking through the mall. She didn't see me. She was carrying a big bag of stuff from the Bon Jon Surf Shop, mostly stuff for herself, I guess. I suddenly felt a little guilty for not buying Posie a present. I almost went back into Afterthoughts to get her some earrings, too, but first I thought I'd see what she was up to. I was about to go up to her and talk to her, but then I noticed this kind of weird look on Posie's face; kind of dreamy, kind of intense. She didn't look like herself. She stopped moving and just stood in the mall for a second, with all the people swirling around her. And then suddenly, she turned around and started walking off in the other direction. Wherever she was going, she looked pretty determined.

So without even meaning to, I started to follow her, and once I started it was pretty hard to just stop, although I felt kind of creepy, like I was stalking her or something. I guess I wanted to see where she was going with that look on her face. The next thing I knew she had gone into Brookstone, and she started walking around looking at all the cool stuff in there. Finally she got this sales guy to help her out. She started looking at all the telescopes in there, and talking to him about each one, and I was thinking, *Who is the telescope for?* I mean it couldn't be for her little sister, Caitlin, and it's not the kind of thing you'd buy your mother. It's definitely a guy present, and I pretty much ruled out her father because Mr. Hoff is about as blind as Ray Charles. I mean, no offense, but he's definitely not the kind of guy you'd buy a telescope for. Then I suddenly remembered what Thorne had said: *Everybody says she's got some new guy, but nobody knows who.*

I guess it's true about Posie having a new boyfriend, and I guess things have gotten very serious. I mean a telescope is a very good present for a guy, and it's not one she'd get for this guy unless things had gone pretty far pretty fast. See, a telescope is exactly the kind of cool gift I always want to buy for people, except I can never think of things like that when I'm shopping. I always resort to books and robes and CDs.

Anyway, I suddenly felt so sad about Posie's new Astronaut Boyfriend, and so ashamed of myself for following her, that I had to just get out of there. So I did. I practically ran all the way back to the car, over an hour before Mom was supposed to meet me. But I didn't want to see anyone or talk to anyone. I just wanted to disappear. The car was locked so I had to sit there on the hood like an idiot.

As I waited, I got out Dad's submarine book and read it. Now I remember. It's called DEFCOM NINE. It sucks.

It's about three-fifteen on Xmas afternoon. We've opened all the presents and eaten scrambled eggs and now it's that kind of dead lull where we're all in our rooms kind of going over our gifts and napping and waiting for the ham to come out of the oven. Mr. Bond is here. He arrived about nine A.M., which I don't mind, I guess, but Mom should have told us he was coming is all I can say. And he should have brought us something—I mean anything, a pack of Slim Jims, whatever—but no, he just shows up and gives Mom this package from Victoria's Secret. And of course, it was a tiger-print panties and bra set. Gross. I can't decide what is more disgusting, Mom wearing that, or Mr. Bond shopping for it. Sorry, I mean *Robere*.

Honey really liked the PJ Harvey CD. When she opened it she said, "Nice choice," and she didn't add a phrase like "Monkey Nuts" or anything, like she usually does, so I could tell she was impressed. Mom said she liked her robe, but I bet she tried on Robere's underwear first. The two of them are in her room now, and if Honey didn't have her new CD on full blast I bet you could hear them.

Christmas is weird. For the last few years it just depressed me because it reminded me of when Mom and Dad were still married. Everything we did, even if it was sort of fun, just reminded me of the kind of family we couldn't be anymore.

This year is kind of sad, too, in a way, because next year Honey is going to be at Harvard. It's really the last year Mom and Honey and I are going to be together like this. I am definitely going to miss Honey next year, although maybe it's only on Christmas that I'd actually admit this.

The house smells like ham.

I got a Game Boy from Mom, which is a nice present I guess, but it also kind of seems like the kind of gift you'd get some kid you don't know very well. It's fine, though, I got Scuba War, too, which is this game where you basically try to kill all these sharks before they eat you. And Honey gave me a new journal with a black cover, just like the ones I always use. I'm only about halfway through this one, but it was a pretty cool gift. She also gave me a nice pen, kind of a fake fountain pen with these little cartridges you snap in so you're actually writing with real ink. The color is this weird blue-green called Peacock Blue, which I also like. So Honey definitely wins the present contest. Thanks, Honey!

And Dad sent a check for a hundred dollars. It came in an envelope addressed in Tiffany's handwriting, and the check was signed by Tiffany, too— Tiffany St. Clair Black. God, it sounds like the name of a porn star. I wonder if Dad got her some tiger panties for Xmas, too. I mean assuming she doesn't already own some, which I bet she does. That's probably all she wears.

Dad hasn't called us yet to say, *Merry Christmas, did you get my check?* He usually does, but maybe he'll call later. We could call him, but he's the one who divorced Mom. I think that means he should make the call.

I wonder what Sophie is doing right now. I'm looking at the earrings I bought her and I can't wait to give them to her. Two days to go! And I wonder if Posie has given that telescope to her new boyfriend. Maybe they're looking through it, and they can see me lying here, writing in my notebook, and I look like somebody really far away.

Just before we ate dinner, I was sitting around the living room watching a football game with my new best friend, Robere. He was drinking a beer, and I could tell he was thinking of offering me one, except that it would be kind of weird for him to offer me a beer in my own house.

"Hey, Joner," he said.

"Hey, Mr. Bond."

He wagged his finger at me, like he was saying, *naughty, naughty*, and I said, "I mean Robere."

"Are you having a good Christmas?" he said.

"Yeah," I said. "It's fine."

"I am. I wanted you to know that," he said. "I'm really enjoying this Christmas."

"I'm glad," I said, keeping my eyes on the TV.

"Seriously." I hate it when people say *seriously* to keep a conversation going that you'd just as soon drop. "It means a lot to have you accept me into your family. That you don't mind having me around."

I decided to let him get away with this, because after all it was Christmas, and why shouldn't I be nice to him? I mean, there's nothing really wrong with Mr. Bond, except for the fact that he's my history teacher, and Thorne's homeroom teacher, and he's sleeping with Mom, and he wants me to call him *Robere*.

"Well, Robere," I said. "I'm glad you're around. I know Mom's happy you're around."

"She's a pretty special lady," Mr. Bond said, and looked back at the bedroom, where Mom was napping. "Yes indeed."

Gross. We watched the game for a little while. Scoreless.

"You know, I was married before," he said.

This was news to me. I wasn't sure why he was telling me this now.

"Yeah?" I said.

"Yes," said Mr. Bond and sighed. "Phan Nguoc."

"Excuse me?" I said.

"Phan Nguoc. That was her name," he said. "She was Vietnamese."

"Oh," I said. "Were you in Vietnam?"

Mr. Bond shrugged. "Nah," he said.

He watched the game for a while, as if the conversation were over, which was weird, since he was the one who'd started it.

"So what happened to her?" I said.

"She had cancer, Jonah," said Mr. Bond. "Breast cancer." And just like that, Mr. Bond's eyes got all watery and these two big tears slid down his cheeks. He wiped his face on the back of his shirt cuff.

"Sorry," he said.

"I'm sorry," I said. "That she died." I thought how incredibly lame it sounded to say this, but I meant it. There wasn't any good way of putting it, I guess.

"Me too," he said. He drank some beer. "You know, for a long time I didn't think I was ever going to get over it." He paused. "Then I met your mom." He looked back at the bedroom. "She sure is special."

The phone started ringing. I waited for someone to answer it.

"Yes," he said, like he was in a trance. "Really special."

I got up and answered the phone.

"Jonah!" said my father. "It's your dad! Your dad, Jonah!"

Dad always sounds like I should be incredibly grateful that he's called. He doesn't seem to have any clue that he's the one who should be grateful we answer.

"Hi, Dad," I said.

"Merry Christmas!" he shouted.

"Merry Christmas to you, too, Dad. We're all just sitting around here—" I said.

"Good, good!" he said. "We've got a fire going. Tiffany and I are going over to the Cricket Club for supper. Thought we'd give you a quick check on the horn, make sure you're full of Yuletide cheer."

"Oh, we've got cheer all over the place, Dad." I think that's about the strangest thing I may have ever said.

"Is your sister there?" he said.

"Yeah, let me get her."

"Wait, wait, Jonah, before you put her on—can I just ask, she's doing okay, isn't she?" he said.

"She's going to Harvard. She got in early decision," I told him.

"She did? Splendid! That's outstanding!" His voice got fainter and I heard him say, "Honor Elspeth got into Harvard." Tiffany said something back, but I couldn't make out the words. I could tell by the tone of her voice she was standing there in one of her little dresses looking at her watch.

"Did this just happen?" Dad asked me.

"She found out about a month ago, I guess," I told him.

"Oh, shucks, I wish she'd called me and told me herself," Dad said. "I'm so proud!"

And I was thinking, *Well, Dad, if you called more often, you would have found out.*

"And your mother, Jonah—I hope you don't mind my asking about your mother. How is she?"

At that moment, Mom came out of the bedroom. She looked good. She was smiling. Her hair was newly brushed. She was wearing lip gloss. I could tell she'd been fixing herself up for a while. "She's great," I said.

"Good, good. Well then. How's the diving? Diving still good?" he asked.

"It's great," I said.

"And you got that check I sent you, didn't you?" he said.

"I did. Thanks, Dad."

"Yes, well, you go out and get yourself something. I don't know. I never know what you need, Jonah," he said.

Exactly, I thought. "Did you get the book?"

"*Defcom Nine*! Yes, thank you, it's outstanding! In fact, I just finished *Defcom Eight* a couple of weeks ago."

"Okay," I said. "Hold on. Let me get Honey."

I put the phone down. "Who's that, Jonah?" said Mom.

"It's Dad."

"Ah," Mom said. Mr. Bond put his arm around her. I went and got Honey, who was lying on her bed, reading and listening to her new CD on her headphones.

"Phone," I said. "It's Dad."

"Really?" said Honey. She swung her feet onto the floor and almost ran out into the hallway to get the phone. I forget that she's younger than me most of the time, but the way she just bounded out of bed to talk to Dad made her seem like a little girl.

The book she had been reading was now open on the bed. *Winnie Ille Pu*. It was *Winnie the Pooh*, in Latin.

I'm kind of restless today. I guess I'm so psyched for tomorrow I don't know what to do. I'm already packed, and I even remembered the condoms. I put them inside this little zippered compartment in my duffel bag. When I put them in there I suddenly thought, *Maybe I am totally off base about what Sophie wants from lying around a hotel room with me.* I mean maybe it's never occurred to her that we're going to be sleeping together. I mean isn't that like, exactly what I saved her from with Sullivan the Giant? And now I'm just zipping the condoms into my bag? Maybe what she really wants to do is just talk, to just lie in bed and tell stories and turn to each other and take our clothes off and listen to the sounds of the pipes in the hotel, all the water rushing to all the rooms, and Christ, I don't know, I don't know, I don't know! She *did* say she'd "waited" for me, though, right? I mean, that sort of means she thinks we're going to sleep together. I even went back and read what I wrote December seventeenth, that time we were on the phone and it sounded like she really wanted to have sex. But did I write down what she said? I mean, it's possible I might have remembered it wrong, or written it down differently. Now I can't even remember what she looks like.

I went out for a bike ride around noon, just trying to get out of the house and clear my head. I headed down to the beach and locked up the bike and climbed the lifeguard stand. I waited for Pops to appear, but he didn't. This struck me as kind of odd, since Pops always seems to magically appear whenever I climb up the lifeguard stand. Then I got this weird feeling like, maybe Pops Berman isn't real. He's like this magic fairy or guardian angel or, I don't know, like, an alien who can make himself look like a little old man—and whenever I need advice I go to the lifeguard tower and *zzaapp*, Pops beams in and tells me to go "walk the doggy."

I sat there for a while and watched the ocean. I thought about my last diving meet. I thought about Mom and Mr. Bond. And Honey and Dad. I thought about college. I thought about Sophie and meeting her tomorrow, and what that will be like. I reached into my pocket, where I'd put her earrings. I've been carrying them around with me. I closed my eyes.

Sophie opens her hotel room door and throws her arms around me.

"Oh, Jonah," she cries. "You can't imagine how bad it is not being with you."

And I say, "It's all right, Sophie, we're together now." I give her the box with the earrings in it and she starts to cry.

"They're perfect, just what I wanted," she breathes. She looks up at me. "Is it all right if I model them for you?"

I go over to the minibar and pour myself a drink. "Yes," I say. "I'd like that."

Slowly, she takes off all of her clothes, piece by piece. First her sweater, then her skirt, then her bra, then her panties, then she takes out the earrings and puts them in her ears. They kind of swing in her hair.

"How do I look?" she says.

And I say, "Perfect."

Finally, I got off the lifeguard stand and decided to walk up to Niagara Towers to maybe wish Pops Berman a Merry Christmas. When I asked for him the woman at the front desk asked me if I'm a member of the family, and I said, "I'm his friend." The receptionist—this very cute Caribbean girl with a sun-and-moon pin on her shirt—said that Pops was in the hospital having dialysis. St. Joseph's, she said.

So I bicycled over there, but they said I couldn't see him, family members only. So I asked them to say Jonah Black had been there and they said, sure. I have no idea whether he got the message or not.

I guess I'm kind of upset about Pops. It's weird how important he is to me even though I don't really know him. I keep thinking about that story he told me about the woman he loved. The one who died. I wonder if my life will end up like that.

When I got back to the house, Mom said that Posie had stopped by. I felt so bad, I couldn't believe I'd missed her. I went into my room and guess what—there on my bed was a gift from Brookstone, all wrapped up in sparkly paper covered with the night sky and stars.

I opened it up. It was the telescope. And a card that said, "For Jonah, a bright planet in a dark sky." I was completely blown away. I still am. I mean this whole time I was thinking she'd gotten the present for some other boyfriend, and her other boyfriend turns out to be me. Then I read her note again and it kind of weirded me out a little, like what does she mean, a bright planet in a dark sky? Like her sky's all dark these days? It made me wonder if she was all right.

I called her up but Mrs. Hoff said, "No, Jonah. Posie isn't here. She left for a few days. College visiting."

Dec. 27, 1:15 P.M.

Well, here we are, Thorne at the wheel of his Beetle, me attempting to write this while Thorne zooms past everyone at ninety miles an hour and Limp Bizkit is blasting on the stereo. Mom kissed me on the cheek this morning just before we left. "I'm proud of you, Jonah," she said, and I suddenly felt like a giant rat, lying to her. Honey looked at me from the doorway of her room while I was being hugged by Mom, and her look said, *You might think you're fooling her but you're not fooling me.*

(Still Dec. 27, 5:30 P.M.)

I am in the Porpoise! I had to give up writing in the car because it was way too bumpy and I couldn't concentrate.

———— ■ ————

Thorne has dropped me off here and is off to UCF. He says he doesn't know where he's staying, but he's totally unconcerned about it. I wish I had Thorne's ability not to worry about things so much.

Now I'm lying on my big king-size bed waiting for Sophie to call. And when she does I will tell her to come to my room and the two of us will lie around and maybe do it.

I'm kind of nervous. Just sitting here writing this my heart is pounding so hard it's actually making my shirt move.

I ran into my first complication when I checked into the hotel. I told them my name and that I was staying for two nights and they said that would be four hundred and seventy-five dollars. I said okay and paid them. But Jesus, this place is expensive! I'm so stupid I didn't even ask how much it was when I booked the room. I guess I'm going to have to get Thorne or someone to loan me some money because I won't even be able to pay to get into Disney World at this rate. Or eat. Or anything.

It's completely possible this is all like, a giant disaster waiting to happen. But I don't care.

(Still Dec. 27, 6:30 P.M.)

Okay, so now it's

Sorry. The doorbell rang just at that second and it was the delivery guy bringing me a pizza. I wanted to say, hey, man, I deliver pizzas, too! But this is a hotel and I'm supposed to be the guest so I didn't say anything. He said, can I put it on the table for you sir, and I said okay, and I tipped him two dollars, which I know is a pretty crummy tip but I'm really worried about money now. I kind of hope Thorne checks in from UCF.

I called the front desk and asked what room the O'Briens were staying in.

The concierge said, "Who?"

And I said, "The O'Briens."

And he goes, "They're guests here, sir?"

I said yes, and there was this long pause as he checked his computer and then he said, "There's no one by that name registered at the hotel."

"Are you sure?" I said.

And he said "Yes, sir," sounding all annoyed.

So I hung up and I realize now I'm sitting in a hotel I can't afford waiting for a girl who might not even show up. Who might not even exist.

I have to say I sort of started to panic, so that's when I ordered the pizza, with everything on it.

Sausages, pepperonis, green peppers, onions, extra cheese. I've been lying here watching MTV while I chow down on pizza and two Cokes and now I feel a little bit better. I'm still panicked, except now I weigh an additional five pounds so it's kind of like I have ballast, or an anchor. Or something.

This hotel room is pretty cool. It's definitely not the usual Howard Johnson with the wood paneling and an oil painting of some hunters shooting geese. Downstairs in the lobby there was this amazing kind of fabric thing hanging from the ceiling, like a big parachute or something. The wind makes it kind of flutter in the breeze and it's really cool. The hotel is huge, too—it goes on forever. There are at least two swimming pools—I haven't actually looked at them yet, but there are pictures in this brochure on the desk that show that they have these weird little water-falls in them, so it's sort of like Typhoon Lagoon.

I guess it's just beginning to hit me that I might be getting stood up here. Like maybe Sophie never intended to come down here at all. Maybe leading me on was all some big joke to her. Or maybe she thought I'd never really do it, rent a room and come see her.

But I talked to her on the phone, and we definitely had a connection or something. I can't believe she'd just lie. She's not a bad person.

Maybe something happened, like she had this

sudden change of plans and she couldn't get in touch with me.

Maybe I should call home and ask Mom if I've gotten any messages. But Mom would be able to tell something is wrong, from my voice. Wouldn't she? I don't know why I think this but I bet she could. Of course, she didn't think there was anything funny going on when I came up with this ridiculous story in the first place. Maybe I could do it without her worrying about anything. I'd have to wait until she's off the air—right now is when she does her stupid radio show.

In fact. Hang on a second.

Okay. I just turned on the radio and of course Mom's show is syndicated in Orlando. So I'm sitting here in a hotel room I've rented in order to meet this girl, and I'm listening to my mother on the radio talking to phone-in callers in Fort Lauderdale. The guy she's talking to right now is asking her if it's okay that he likes to have sex in the car better than in the bed.

And mom says, *Are you being n*

(Still Dec. 27, 10:25 P.M.)

All right. I'm back, after kind of an adventure. The phone rang right in the middle of Mom asking, *Are you being nice to yourself?* and I practically knocked the lamp over trying to get to it.

Instead of Sophie, though, it was Thorne. He wanted me to come to this party at UCF with "all of his friends," and I thought, *Thorne, man, you've been on campus for about five hours—how can you have "friends" already?* He asked about Sophie and I had to tell him the truth. And of course, Thorne swung into action.

"Okay, Jonah. Now you've *got* to come to this gig. Be in front of the hotel in a half hour, I'll come get you."

"But Thorne—Sophie's supposed to call here," I said.

"Exactly," Thorne said. "You want *her* to wait for *you*, Jonah, not the other way around. You get yourself out of there, hang out with some of these college chicks. If you want Sophie to call you, the only way now is for you not to be there."

"Wait," I said. "You're saying that if I stay here, she won't call? And if I leave, she will? How will she know if I'm here or not if she doesn't call?"

"Jonahman," Thorne said. "You still don't get women, do you?"

I didn't say anything.

"They're psychic," Thorne said.

"But if Sophie's so psychic, why doesn't she call when I'm here?" I protested.

"Jonah, you been drinking the Stupid Sauce again? She won't call when you're there because she knows you're waiting around for her! No chick wants to be with a guy who doesn't have any other options! They want you to have your choice of any girl in the world, and then for you to choose *them*. Get it?" he said.

"But how does she know I'm waiting around for her?" I said.

"You are, aren't you? She can tell that. She's not going to call you while you're waiting around for her to call you!" he declared.

"Thorne, this is stupid."

"Exactly. So get the hell out of there. She'll leave a message with reception, you'll call her back later, and then *she'll* be the one with the sweaty palms, wondering when *you* are going to call *her*."

"I thought you said she was psychic," I said.

"Yeah, well, she is. But remember, with chicks there's a fine line between psychic and psycho. You keep her guessing, man. That's the key. Listen. I'll be there in twenty-nine minutes. Be there, dude."

So that's how about an hour later I found myself standing around this keg at an off-campus party in the Orlando suburbs. I think Thorne and I were the youngest people there, just about. I'd never been in a frat house before. There were posters on all the walls and different music coming from every room, and the kitchen was just completely disgusting. Like, there was rotting fruit in a bowl, and beer cans all over the place, and lots of stuff spilling out of the cupboards like weird bags of rice and oatmeal and what looked like little baggies of pot, but maybe they were just herbs. In one corner were a dozen empty pizza boxes. They were the exact same ones that Mr. Swede uses, with the picture of the Italian baker on the front making an "OK" sign with his fingers and smelling the aroma rising from the pie.

There were about a hundred people there, and the music was *really* loud. At the parties in Pompano, the neighbors are right next door, so you can't be that loud or you'll get them mad. But this house had a pretty big yard. I guess you have to be kind of an idiot to live right next to a frat house anyway.

Thorne pretty much disappeared the second we got there. He's already bonded with a bunch of people in the e-business program and they've been showing him around like he's one of the guys. There's this guy Thaddeus who looks like a beach volleyball player or something, but he turns out to be some sort of computer whiz. And this other guy Bruce who barely talks, he just slaps you on the back every five minutes and stares off into space. I guess he's probably on something. Thorne introduced me to them, but once they found out that I'm only a high school junior they pretty much lost interest.

I wound up standing around the keg, because it seemed like a good place to be. Seriously, though, I felt like a loser. It was that weird feeling I get sometimes when I realize one of the loneliest places in the world can be in a room filled with people I don't know.

That's when this guy started talking to me. He was a lot older than me—at first I thought maybe he was a UCF graduate student, but then I realized he was too old even for that. He was practically Mom's age, except that he was wearing these Joe College clothes that made him look younger, at least at first. The longer I looked at him, the sadder he seemed. He looked like someone's drunk uncle.

"Name's Bywater," he said, shaking my hand. "Who are you?"

"Jonah Black," I said. "Your name's really Bywater?" I didn't want to insult him, but it sounded like a pretty stupid name.

"Professor Bywater," he said, as if he were partly proud of this, and partly ashamed. He sort of turned my hand forty-five degrees while he shook it. "Glad to meet you. So you're one of the prospectives?"

"One of the what?" I said.

"Prospectives. One of the folks applying to UCF?" he said.

"Oh," I said. "No. I'm just here with a friend." There was something about this guy I couldn't figure out. He wasn't really looking at me while he was talking. He was glancing around the party at all the girls.

This girl with black curly hair and huge breasts walked by. She was wearing a tube top, and she was really drunk.

"What do you think of that action?" he said. "I tell you, kid, UCF's a great place to scope out the tuna!"

I didn't even know what he was talking about for a second, then I realized this was some sort of '80s lingo for looking at girls. It was kind of a gross thing to say, I thought, especially for a professor.

"You like English?" Professor Bywater asked me.

"It's all right," I said.

"Good man," he said. "It helps you find the answers, doesn't it? Helps you ask the questions."

Professor Bywater kind of swayed back and forth. He had definitely been drinking—a lot. "Listen," I said. "I gotta go." I figured it'd be better for all concerned if I just got the hell away from this guy. He was seriously depressing me.

"I remember when I was your age," he said. It sounded like he was about to say something else, but he didn't.

"What do you remember?" I felt like I had to ask him.

"Wanting to get laid," he said.

"That's it?" I asked. "That's all you remember?"

"Jonah, tell me what you're reading in English right now. You're at a wonderful age, reading all the great works for the first time."

"I don't know. *To Kill a Mockingbird*." Actually, we'd read that in seventh grade, but I figured it would shut him up. Why I thought this I don't know, because it didn't.

"Harper Lee!" he shouted. "'*You never really know a man until you've walked around in his shoes.*' Do you think that's true, Jonah?"

"I don't know," I said.

"I think you know it's true," said Professor Bywater. "I think you've spent a lot of time walking in other people's shoes." He took off his Wallabees and shoved them toward me. "Go on. Take a walk."

"I'm not kidding," I said. "I really do have to go."

"Let me tell you something," Professor Bywater said. He put one of his hands on my shoulder. He was looking at me over the top of his half-frame glasses. "And I'm only telling you this because we're kindred spirits, you and I, aren't we? Two peas in a pod."

"I'm okay, really," I said.

"It's the secret of life. You ready?" he asked me.

"I said I'm okay," I repeated. I was now officially freaked out by this guy.

"Find a girl, Jonah," he whispered. *"A girl."*

"Okay. Fine," I said.

"You find a girl, Jonah, and worship her."

"Okay," I said. "Thanks for the tip."

"You play sports?" he said. "You do. I can tell."

"I'm on the diving team."

"I used to be a diver," he whispered, and his bad breath blasted me in the face. It smelled like coleslaw gone sour. "I was a very good diver."

Enough already with this guy. "That's great," I said, and walked away.

I could still smell his breath on my face and I felt sort of shaky. Professor Bywater was seriously scary. From across the room, I turned around and I could see him talking to someone else, a young college girl. I could tell from the look on her face she thought he was nuts, too. Man, I thought. What a pathetic jerk. Hanging around the frat house at age forty trying to pick up girls.

And then I had this horrible thought. *You see that guy?* I thought. *That could be you in twenty years.*

I kind of stunned myself with this thought, and then I was like, what kind of stupid thing is that to tell yourself? I'm not Professor Bywater. I'm not even a potential Professor Bywater. Except for the diving thing, we have nothing in common. Maybe Professor Bywater isn't a professor at all. He's just some lunatic who calls himself a professor and everyone tolerates him because in general, people are pretty nice. I don't know. I hope I never see him again is all I can say.

The good part of this story is that a moment later the girl he'd been talking to came over to me and smiled, and there was something natural and real and unforced about it. She had straight brown hair and very pale skin and a small mole just above her mouth.

"Do you think he's okay?" I said.

"You know what? I don't care," she said. "I'm rather hoping he isn't okay. He's a creep." She smiled that smile again. "My name's Molly Beale," she said. "Who are you?"

"Jonah Black."

"You know what I was wondering, Jonah Black, when that loser unleashed himself on me? I was just wondering if this college party scene is all bullshit or what. What's your theory on that question?"

She said this in a completely honest way. It

sounded like that's really what she was doing at that second, going over in her mind whether or not this whole party was bullshit.

"I don't know, I'm new here," I said.

"I'm new here, too. I don't go to college. I'm in high school. I'm just looking at all these college kids wondering what's the deal with them." She looked around curiously. "I mean is it just me, or is everyone here basically kind of drunk and stupid?"

I laughed. "You know, now that you mention it, everyone here *is* kind of drunk and stupid," I said.

"Except us, of course," said Molly.

"Of course." I shrugged. "I don't go here, either. I'm in eleventh grade at Don Shula High, down in Pompano Beach."

"No way," Molly said. "I'm from Lauderdale-by-the-Sea. I'm a junior at St. Winnifred's."

I couldn't believe it. Out of the blue I suddenly find this cute girl who actually seems normal. "I know somebody who goes to school there," I said.

"Who?"

"Elanor Brubaker?"

"Oh, her," she said, and it was clear just how little time Molly had for Elanor Brubaker in her life.

"I know somebody she used to go out with," I clarified.

"Who, Loverboy over there?" She nodded at

114

Thorne, who was drinking beer through a funnel. Bruce and Thaddeus and their buddies were cheering him on. Thorne finished the funnel, smacked his lips, grabbed the nearest girl and kissed her on the lips. Everyone cheered even louder and Thorne kept on kissing her. The girl wasn't even blushing.

"Yeah," I said.

"Well, Elanor is so full of crap it's not funny," Molly said. She pushed her brown hair behind her ears with her ring fingers. It was this incredibly cool, delicate gesture. "But that guy Thorne is even worse. He's like a walking baloney sandwich."

I laughed. "Yeah. I guess that's what people find so endearing about him."

"Is that right?" she said. Her hair fell back down again. "Which people are these?"

I laughed. "I don't know."

She said something I couldn't hear, but I nodded anyway. It was actually a little hard to hear her over the music.

"So why are you here?" I said. "If you don't go to school here?"

She smiled at me. "Why are *you?*"

"It's kind of a long story," I said.

"Yeah, well, the St. Winnifred's choir is singing Handel's *Messiah* here. That's my story. Nice and short."

"You're in the choir?"

She started singing. *"And His name shall be called Wonderful, Counsellor, the Mighty God, the Everlasting Father, the Prince of Peace."* She had a terrible voice. I figured her school choir must be the kind you don't have to audition for to get in.

"So let's get back to guys," she said. "And how full of crap they are."

"Okay. Whatever," I said.

"Why is that?" she said. "I mean is it on purpose, do you think? Or is it just an accident?"

"I don't know," I said. "I think maybe it's because they're afraid."

She looked at me hard. "That's an interesting answer, Jonah Black," she said. "You're saying guys lie to girls because they're afraid. What are they afraid of?"

I thought about it. I wasn't sure I knew the answer. Molly was kind of intense. "I'm not sure. Maybe they're afraid of being rejected."

"Rejected? Why would they be rejected?"

"Because we aren't cool enough. Or something."

"Not cool enough," Molly said. She put her hair behind her ear again. "That's interesting. But what if coolness isn't what girls want from guys?"

"That would be news to me," I said.

"Nevertheless," Molly said. "Maybe what girls want is the truth."

"Which is what exactly?" I was beginning to think this conversation was way too smart for me. I wondered if this was the way all the girls talked at St. Winnifred's.

"The truth?" Molly said. "You're asking me what the truth is? Like you don't know?"

"I'm saying I think it's hard sometimes to tell people who you really are," I said. I wasn't even sure if that was what I meant to say.

"And why is that?" she said.

"Because sometimes you don't know who you really are?" I answered.

"Ah," said Molly. "You're interesting, Jonah Black. You haven't looked at my boobs yet, either."

I really wanted to look at them then, but I couldn't.

"I didn't think it would be polite," I said. I finished the beer I was drinking in one gulp.

"You know, I'm thinking maybe you and I should sit down someplace and have a conversation where we don't have to shout over this imbecilic music. You agree with me, right, that this music would only appeal to morons?" Molly said.

"It sucks," I said. "It definitely sucks."

"In fact, I'm noticing there is a couch over there with imitation zebra-skin upholstery which is currently unoccupied. What would happen if the two of us were to sit down on that couch and converse?"

I was going to need another beer if I was going to keep talking to this Molly girl.

"I don't know." I shrugged.

"Tell you what, I'm going to go and visit what my mother would refer to as the Little Girls' Room, and then let's the two of us recline on that zebra-skin davenport over there and continue our analysis. Does that sound like a good way to proceed?"

"You're a nut, aren't you?" I said to her.

She shrugged. "We shall see, won't we?" Molly turned her back on me and walked through the party. I felt a drop of sweat trickle down my temple. There was something completely direct about her. She had a nice butt, too, I noticed as she walked away. And she was pretty tall. I think I like Molly Beale.

At that moment, these two girls sat down on the zebra-skin couch. I wanted to rush right over and tell them, excuse me, this seat is reserved, but I didn't.

Because one of them was POSIE.

My heart started pounding in my chest. I couldn't believe she was there. I looked around to see if her new mystery boyfriend was with her, but I didn't see anybody. I didn't recognize the girl she was talking to, either. What was Posie doing at a UCF frat party, anyway?

Then I remembered her mother saying Posie was going college visiting. But Jesus, did the college have to be UCF?

I thought about the last time we'd been together, how I'd called her Sophie by accident. I thought about the telescope she'd given me.

Then I turned and ducked out the kitchen door and stood outside in the yard for a second. The grass was littered with plastic cups. A big yellow dog was sleeping under a tree. It raised its head and looked at me. I wondered if I was going to be sick. I can't believe my own life, sometimes.

It's like I'm a cartoon character who's just been hit on the head with a frying pan, and a big bump comes out of the middle of his head and all these stars and moons are circling in the air above him. Except instead of stars and moons, maybe I've got girls.

Suddenly, there was someone behind me, and I thought, *Please, let it be Posie. Please.* Then I thought, *Please let it* not *be Posie.* Then I thought, *Please let it be Molly.* Then I thought, *Please let it* not *be Molly.* Then I thought . . .

"Come on, Jonahboy," said Thorne. "Why don't I take you back to the hotel?"

"No, it's okay, I'm just—" I looked up at him. I guess I looked pretty bad.

"Hey. It's all right. I get it. I'll just drop you off

there and then I'll come back," Thorne said. His voice sounded almost gentle, for him.

"You're sure?"

Thorne nodded. He was strangely serious. We walked to his car and headed back to the Porpoise.

"You didn't tell me Posie was going to be here," I said.

"I didn't know," Thorne said.

"Did she see me? Does she know what I'm doing here?"

"I don't think so," Thorne said. "If she asks me, I'll come up with something."

"It kind of freaked me out, seeing her," I told him.

"Yeah," Thorne said. "I noticed."

We drove for a while in silence. I was grateful Thorne wasn't making me talk. And that he'd left the party to drive me back to the hotel. He's a good guy.

"So who was that chick you were talking to?" he said, when we were close to the hotel.

"Her name's Molly Beale," I said.

"Molly Beale," Thorne said, letting the name roll off his tongue. "Very interesting."

We got back to the hotel, and I got out. "I'm gonna give you one last tip," he said. "If you got a message from Sophie? Don't call her back right away."

"Don't?" I said.

"Nope," he said. "Remember. Make 'em wait."

"Okay," I said. "I'll make her wait."

"You aren't listening to me, are you, Jonahboy?" he said.

"Nope."

"Okay. I'll call you tomorrow," he said. "Have a good night. Later."

Thorne took off in his Beetle, leaving me alone in front of the Porpoise. Flags were flying from poles by the swimming pools. It was dark and there were stars out.

I was glad I had a friend like Thorne.

I walked up to my room. There, by the bed, was the phone. And the message light on it was blinking on and off.

I ran across the room, picked up the phone and hit the button. I hadn't even closed the door. The automated voice said, "One message, delivered ten-fifteen P.M." That was less than ten minutes ago. I waited for the message, and as I waited I thought about what Thorne had said. *Make 'em wait.*

The message started. There was the sound of a room, a television playing in the background somewhere. I could hear someone breathing. She inhaled, then exhaled. Someone in the background said something, but I couldn't figure out what. Then the line went dead.

What if that was Sophie? Is that the last I'll ever hear from her? Or is this just the beginning?

I think I'm in trouble.

Okay, so I just called home to see if there were any messages, and fortunately—or unfortunately—Honey answered the phone. She said Mom was with Mr. Bond and she was "indisposed."

"Listen," I said. "Have there been any messages for me?"

"What's wrong, Llama Nuts, you sound like you're in trouble."

"I said, have there been any messages for me?" I repeated.

"You're calling from Orlando," Honey said. "Where are you, a hotel?"

"How do you know that?" I demanded.

"Caller ID," she said matter-of-factly. "So you did go to Orlando after all. Oh, for crying out loud, Jonah, you aren't meeting her at Disney World, are you?"

I just sat there for a second, amazed at Honey. Is there anything she can't figure out? I guess I shouldn't have been so shocked—I mean she does speak six languages and all. Still, I kind of hate the way I can't keep anything a secret from her.

"Yeah, I'm meeting her at a hotel, Honey," I admitted. "And she isn't here. The front desk says there isn't even anybody by that name registered. I think I'm being stood up."

"Yeah," Honey said. "Sounds like it." It sounded like she thought this was funny. Like I was the most gullible sucker known to man.

"Will you call me if she leaves a message at home?" I said.

"You want me to call you?" she said. "Sure, I'll call you. Give me the number."

"You want me to wait so you can get a pencil or something?"

"I'll remember it," she said. Of course, Honey has a photographic memory. She can tell you the first names of the parents of the kids who were in her kindergarten class eleven years ago.

I gave her the number and then she said, "Listen, Scrote, you don't sound good. Is Thorne with you?"

"No, he's at a party at UCF," I told her.

"When's he coming back?" Honey said.

"I think tomorrow, but I don't know. We left it kind of loose," I said. Even I could hear the note of pathetic desperation in my voice. What a sad character I'm turning out to be.

"Yeah, it sounds pretty loose all right," Honey

said. "You have enough money to pay for that place? It's got to be two-fifty a night."

"I'm fine," I said. "I've got money."

"Huh," she said, clearly not believing me. "Imagine that."

"Okay," I said. "I guess I better go."

"Yeah, well. Have a good time, kid," said Honey. "Enjoy your pizza."

She hung up.

Sometimes I hate my sister.

(Still Dec. 27, almost midnight)

Still waiting for Sophie.

I just did something kind of stupid. I decided to see what was on television and the first thing I got when I switched it on was this ad for Univision. It's that hotel room pay-per-view thing, and most of the movies they have I've either seen, or don't want to see. But then I noticed they had two porno films available, *Busty Backdoor Nurses* and *Sorority Girls*.

I'd never seen an actual porno movie, so I thought, well, what the hell. I mean I want to see what it's like and maybe it would get me out of this depressing mood I'm in. Help me forget about Sophie and that scary professor at the party and the

———— ■ ————

cute girl I messed things up with before we even got to know each other—Molly Beale. I mean maybe it wouldn't make me feel better, but I thought it might be kind of funny.

So I pushed the buttons and went through the menu and soon *Sorority Girls* was starting. It was pretty much exactly what I expected. I guess nobody watches these things for the acting.

The movie hadn't been on for more than a minute when I started getting kind of nervous because I suddenly thought, hey, what happens if Sophie comes over right while I'm watching this? So I tried to put the TV on "off" for a second, just to prove that I could get out of *Sorority Girls* in a hurry if I had to, but the remote didn't work. So then I got up and tried to turn off the TV manually, but none of the buttons seemed to work. It was like I was stuck watching *Sorority Girls.* Only two minutes into it everybody was naked and doing stuff that was really kind of gross. But it was kind of hard not to watch.

Anyway, I figured, worst case scenario, I unplug the set.

So I went back to the bed and kept on watching it. There was this one girl who had a huge birthmark shaped like a fan on her stomach. And all the guys were really geeky-looking, with Coke-bottle glasses and pocket protectors and khakis and loafers and plaid shirts. But when they took off their clothes they were actually these huge steroid-pumped guys with orange fake tans. They stood around acting all shy and uncomfortable and the girl with the birthmark was like, "Don't be shy, come lie down."

Sophie moves over on the bed and I lie down next to her. She runs her fingers down the side of my body and it tickles. She licks my neck.

Right when I was getting into the movie, the phone rang. And I was like, *Sophie*?!

My heart was racing. I went over to the set and tried to turn down the volume, but I couldn't get the controls to work. The phone was ringing and ringing, and I still hadn't answered. What if Sophie hung up while I was messing with the television, trying to turn down the volume on *Sorority Girls*? Could I be more of a loser? So I ran over and picked up the phone, just praying she wouldn't figure out what I was watching.

"Hello?" I said.

"Hey, Peanut," Honey said. "I just wanted to find out how your dream date's going."

"My dream date?" I said. I paused for only a second, trying to think of what to tell her. That was long enough for Honey.

"Jesus," she said. "What the hell are you listening to?"

126

"Nothing," I said. I tried to stretch the cord toward the bathroom so I could turn on the faucet and cover up the moaning sounds coming from the TV, but it wasn't long enough.

"Oh, for Christ's sake, Butterball, you're not watching pornos on pay-per-view, are you?"

"Were you calling for any particular reason, or did you just want to torture me?" I said bitterly.

"Hey! That sounds like *Sorority Girls*, Honey said. "Is that what you're watching? That's a pretty good one. I know one of the chicks in that movie."

"No, you don't," I said.

"Yeah, I do. The chick with the birthmark. That's Elissa St. Susan. Her real name's Gertrude. She goes to St. Luke's. Or she used to, anyway." Honey giggled. "My big brother, all alone, watching *Sorority Girls* in some Disney hotel."

"I have to go," I said.

"Hey, it's nothing to be ashamed of," Honey said. "I kind of figured you'd be into the porno by now. Hey, there's a good lesbo scene coming up. You'll really like it!"

"I'm hanging up," I said, and did.

I went across the room and unplugged the set. It fell silent. I went back and collapsed on the bed. I put my head in the crook of my arm.

At that moment, the clock radio by the bed went

off. I guess the person who stayed in the room before me had set it. The radio was still tuned to Mom's radio show, so there was Mom's voice, filling my hotel room.

"Are you being nice to yourself?" she asked.

I reached over and I pulled the radio plug out of the wall. I can't believe it. Here I am, trying to get together with the girl of my dreams, but she's standing me up, and my sister and my mother are practically stalking me. In my next life I want to be a fish so I can hide underwater and not talk to anyone.

Dec. 28, 8:35 A.M.

Still no Sophie. I feel like such a loser.

I think what I might have to do this morning is call her house in Maine and see if she's there.

If her parents answer, I'm hanging up.

(Still Dec. 28, 8:44 A.M.)

Okay, so I just called her house in Maine, and guess what? There was no answer. I sat on the edge of the bed, feeling my heart pounding, and listening to a phone ring like, thousands of miles away. My finger was above the clicker ready to hang up that second in case her father answered the phone, but it just rang and rang. There wasn't even an answering machine, which is pretty weird. But I guess nothing about Sophie is what I expected.

So I'm back in the Twilight Zone, I guess.

What do I do now? Should I sit around the hotel room all day, waiting for the phone to ring? Should I go lie by the pool and just check my messages every once in a while? Should I find Thorne and head home?

If I had any brains I'd pick option number three.

(Still Dec. 28, 11 A.M.)

So I just called Dr. LaRue. I dialed his "after hours" number, and I was thinking, Wow, if I'm calling Dr. LaRue I'm probably in more trouble than I'm admitting to myself. Still, it felt good to have somebody I could call.

So I told the doctor what was going on and he didn't seem surprised at all. It was almost as if getting myself into this stupid situation was exactly what he expected from me.

"Do you want me to come up there and get you, Jonah?" he offered. I thought that was a pretty generous thing for Dr. LaRue to say, especially considering that I usually treat him like he's an idiot.

"No, I'm okay. Thorne'll give me a ride home," I said.

"Do you want me to call your mom for you?" he said.

That was the last thing I wanted. "No, I'm really all right," I insisted. "I just thought I should talk to somebody. This is all pretty weird."

"It sounds like you're feeling disappointed, Jonah," Dr. LaRue said.

"Yeah. You could say that."

"Why do you think you're disappointed?" he asked me.

"Because Sophie turned out to be such a flake. Because she said she'd meet me here and instead I'm just lying around this hotel room and I'm totally bored."

"Those are good reasons," said Dr. LaRue. In the background, I thought I heard water running. I wondered what he was doing. Did he have the phone in the bathroom with him? "Are there other reasons you're disappointed?" he asked. "Besides being disappointed with Sophie?"

The water kept tinkling quietly in the background and I thought, *Whoa. Don't tell me Dr. LaRue is* peeing *while he's talking to me?*

"Jonah?" Dr. LaRue said.

"I'm here." That fluid sound was still going and I was starting to feel pissed off at Dr. LaRue for not concentrating on me. He should have just put the phone down. He could have said, *Excuse me for a moment, Jonah*, or something. I'd have waited. It's not like I had a whole lot else to do.

The toilet flushed. I couldn't believe it. My shrink peed while he was talking to me. How nasty is that?

"I asked you if there are other reasons you're disappointed," Dr. LaRue said.

"Yeah. I'm disappointed in myself," I said. I knew it was what he wanted me to say. I just wanted to get off the phone.

"Good, Jonah," he said. "Good."

"So what are you going to do now?" I heard water rushing in the sink. The doc was washing his hands now. I'd had enough of this.

"You know what I'm going to do?" I said, and then I hung up on him.

I went over to the mirror hanging above the shiny hotel dresser and I took a good look at myself.

"You know what I'm going to do?" I said again. "I'm going to the Magic Kingdom."

(Still Dec. 28, 4:30 P.M.)

Okay. Back now from a long day in the Magic Kingdom. I left the hotel and got a shuttle bus over to the park, and by noon I was there.

I love Disney World. Either I forgot how much I loved it when I was a kid or maybe now I just have a whole new perspective on things, but being there really lifted my spirits. The very first thing I did was to go to the Haunted House, which was always my favorite when I was little. It was so cool! I almost forgot about Sophie and this stupid situation I'm in. Even waiting in line was cool. I'd forgotten what that was like, too, how you spend hours in the Magic Kingdom just standing around. It gave me time to think. Actually it gave me time to not think. And then when we got into the Haunted House there was the cool trick where you get into the "locked room," which is really an elevator, and the pictures on the wall start to grow and the next thing you know, you're moving on those little cars and going through the mansion. There is so much to look at, you can't see it all. And I love the disembodied heads singing in the graveyard.

Anyway, this bizarre thing happened. As I was going through the big haunted ballroom, for just a second my car spun around and I saw, in a car a few rows ahead of me, Posie and her sister Caitlin! They didn't see me, and a second later my car spun into a different position again, and I wasn't even sure if was them.

I thought about how I'd seen Posie at the UCF party, and I wondered if she'd run into Thorne when he went back to the party after dropping me off. I could imagine Posie and Molly Beale sitting down on a couch together, talking about me. About what a jerk I am.

Anyway, when my car was on its way out we passed through the kind of funny place where you can see yourself in a mirror and there's a ghost in your car, and I was surprised by my own reflection. I looked so miserable I didn't even recognize myself at first.

Then I got out and went over to the Pirates of the

Okay, it's about five minutes later and the phone just rang. It was Thorne.

"UCF is wild, Jonahman. Out of control. College is going to be one big stinkin' party," he said.

"Listen, Thorne, I gotta ask you. Did you see Posie at the party when you got back? Was she still there?"

"Posie? Nah. She'd taken off. I tell you though, it wouldn't be a bad thing if some of the chicks at our school learned some of the things that these UCF chicks know."

"Like what?" I said.

"Like crazy stuff you're too young to know about, Mr. Studly. Anyway, listen, Jonah. I'm not gonna meet you at the hotel tonight, okay? I'm into some serious business here," he said.

"What do you mean, serious?" I said.

"Serious!" said Thorne, but the way he said it, it didn't sound very serious.

"I'll pick you up tomorrow, okay?"

"Okay," I said.

Then there was a pause, and Thorne said, "Sophie never called, did she?"

"No," I said. I almost felt like crying.

Thorne sighed. "Well, the hell with her. Even if she calls you now, I wouldn't talk to her. You can't be jumping through hoops like a trained seal, all right my man? You have to let her know you won't stand for this BS, dude."

"Yeah, I guess," was all I said. After that, I hung up.

Now I'm back to writing and waiting for room service to show up with a plate of nachos I can't afford.

After the Haunted House I went over to Pirates of the Caribbean. I've always loved the pirate ship and the fire, but I'd forgotten about that one guy who chases the pirate wench girl around and around in a circle. I was like, look that's me! I keep going around and around in a circle and no matter how close I get, the girl keeps running in the other direction.

I remember walking up to Sophie this one time when she was sitting in the art room, painting. She looked like she was crying, or trying not to. And the painting was of a blond girl standing on the edge of a cliff, about to jump off. I didn't know what to say, but I wanted to say something.

"Who's going to save her?" I said, finally.

And Sophie said in this really dreamy sad voice, "No one can, she has to jump."

I think maybe that was when I fell in love with her, because I wanted to be the one to save her. And in a way, that's exactly what did happen. I saved her from Sullivan.

I guess I like saving people—not that it's ever gotten me anywhere.

I remember one time when Honey and I were about the same age as when we went looking for Toby's grave, we were swimming at the public swimming pool and it was really crowded. It was a humid summer day, and we were playing Marco Polo in the water. These bigger kids were throwing a Frisbee around above our heads. Anyway, I was stumbling around the pool blindfolded saying, "Marco," and Honey was saying "Polo." Of course, even then she was a genius and no matter how close I thought I was, the next time she said "Polo" she was in a totally different place.

And then I heard this kind of clunking sound, and I said, "Marco," and nobody said anything back. So I said, "Marco," again and nobody said anything. I felt scared all of a sudden, so I pulled off the blindfold and there was Honey, kind of floating in the water. I think the big kids' Frisbee had hit her on the side of her head and it just knocked her cold. The lifeguard didn't even notice. He was just this big kid with a zinc-oxide nose sleeping in his chair.

So I pulled Honey over to the shallow end and laid her on the stairs, and I was about to try to do mouth-to-mouth resuscitation when she kind of came around. I guess she figured out pretty quickly what had happened, because she dove down under the water and swam over to the deep end and ripped the Frisbee out of this one guy's hand and smacked him on the head with it.

That's the only time I ever rescued anybody besides Sophie. It's funny, I don't know if Honey even remembers that. I'll have to ask her about it sometime when she isn't being too obnoxious. But it'll probably be like that story about Toby's grave—I bet Honey remembers it a totally different way. I wonder how Sophie remembers that night after the dance when I saved her from Sullivan. She probably has a completely different take on it.

I wonder if Betsy Donnelly was right when she

tried to warn me off Sophie. I never responded to that letter she wrote me, which was kind of mean, I guess. I just didn't want to hear bad stuff about Sophie.

I wonder what Betsy would think if I called her up right now. I have a perfect excuse, too, since here I am getting stood up by Sophie, and Betsy knew all along she couldn't be trusted.

Okay, I just dialed the number in the Masthead girls' dorm and the phone is ringing. Betsy's e-mail said she was staying there over Christmas break, which is really kind of sad, actually. The phone is still ringing.

Betsy's going to answer the phone in a minute. "Sophie didn't show?" she'll say.

"Nope," I'll say. "But I was wondering if you could make it down here, Bets. I miss you."

"I miss you, too," she'll say. Then she'll hop the next plane and knock on my door and we'll watch pay-per-view all night and lie around and take showers.

Now it's a few seconds later. A girl answered the phone.

It was Sophie's voice!

"Hello?" I said. "Sophie?"

"Sophie?" the voice said, and this time it didn't sound like her. "You've got the wrong number, okay?"

"Sophie, is that you?"

—— ▪ ——

"Don't call back here again! I'm not kidding!" she said, and the line went dead.

And now I'm lying here wondering if that really was Sophie who answered the phone. Maybe she stayed there over Christmas, too. Or maybe it was Betsy, or a wrong number, or maybe I'm freaking out.

I think I need to get out of here, but someone's knocking on the door.

I'm not getting too excited. It's just my nachos.

(Still Dec. 28, 9 P.M.)

Now I'm down in the bar eating pretzels.

I don't know. I guess I've been made a fool of. Or, as Pops Berman says, a "total idiot."

But maybe it's all for the best, because I think I'm beginning to come to my senses and realize how stupid this all was. I need to concentrate on reality from now on, on diving and getting through this school year and senior year and applying to college. I can't be mooning around about some girl who doesn't even take me seriously, who thinks I'm just some joker she can lie to.

I wonder what Mom's going to be like next year, with Honey gone to Harvard. Is it going to be hard for her, with her daughter out of the house? In a way, I can almost forgive Mom for acting like such a freak these days. These are freaky times.

I guess I can almost forgive everybody. Life is so damned complicated, it's amazing more people don't just flip out.

I still keep thinking about Pops Berman, and that girl he was in love with. I hope Pops is okay when I get back.

---■---

Okay, I'm up, and I'm down in the hotel restaurant. I just finished a stack of pancakes after what was maybe the most bizarre night of my life. It's happened. I've seen her.

Wait, I want to make sure I get this all down exactly right.

Okay. It started about one A.M. last night, when the phone rang in my room.

"Jonah?"

"It's me," I said. "Sophie?"

"Yes, it's Sophie," she said.

"Sophie! My God, where are you?" I nearly shouted.

It was really her this time. No fooling.

"We're at the Dolphin. I got mixed up, you

141

know? Porpoise, Dolphin, whatever. Are you okay?"
she said. She didn't sound especially worried or
sorry about the mix-up.

"Yeah, I'm great," I said. But I was also thinking, *Well, it would have been nice if you'd called
earlier.*

"Can I come over there?" Sophie asked me. She
was kind of whispering, and I wondered if she was
trying to have this conversation while her parents
were asleep in the same room with her. Or her little
sister or someone.

"Sure," I said. "Now?" I looked at the clock.

"Yeah. I'll be there in about twenty minutes. Is
that okay? What room are you in?"

"I'm in 201-J."

"Okay. I'll be right over."

And then, at one-forty A.M., Sophie O'Brien walked
into my room. She knocked softly and I opened the
door and there she was—*Sophie.* Her hair was just as
I remembered it, maybe a little longer.

"Jonah?" she said uncertainly. "Jonah Black?"

She wasn't sure it was me. I nodded. It was me
all right.

She reached out and hugged me. The door
swung shut and she pressed herself against me,
this amazing girl with her body against mine. Then
she tilted her head back and our lips found each

other and we kissed for a long time. It was like a glass of lemonade on the hottest day of summer. It was like a blast of cold wind on top of a mountain. It was like chocolate and loud music and doing a triple somersault off the high board.

We made our way over to the bed and I sat down on the end of it and looked at her. She was wearing a thin little sundress, white with faint yellow stripes on it, and it was dotted all over with these red bursts of color, like flowers or fireworks or something. I could see her blue bra through the silky material. Her hair was full of color, too—mostly blond, but with a few reddish-brown streaks. She wasn't wearing any makeup except for this rose-colored lipstick, and she was kind of nervously twisting her long hair into a braid over one shoulder.

"I'm so sorry," she whispered. "I'm such an idiot."

"No, you're not. You're amazing," I said.

"No," she said, and sat down on the bed next to me. I just looked into her eyes, drinking her in. She was really there! She was really real!

"You're the one who's amazing. I've been waiting for so long to thank you for what you did. I mean, you totally got kicked out of school for me, didn't you? I still don't know how to thank you."

"You already have," I said.

"I tell you what, Jonah Black," she said, and

143

her face got all serious and dark. It was almost scary. "I'm going to do you a favor someday, too. Okay?"

"Sophie, you don't owe me anything."

"I'm not kidding," she said, with this scary face that really gave me the creeps. "Someday, my debt to you will be paid. Okay?"

"Okay," I said. "Whatever."

And just like that, the cloud passed from her face and she looked normal again. She smiled at me. "God," she said. She looked me up and down. "Look at you!"

"Look at you," I said back.

She just laughed, but her laugh wasn't cute and giggly. It was a sad laugh. Older than her years.

"What happened?" I said. "I thought we said yesterday."

"Did we?" she said. She shrugged and smiled at me. "Whatever." She looked around the room. "Man, all hotel rooms are pretty much the same deal, aren't they?"

"Yeah," I said, although I haven't actually been in that many.

"How do you feel? Nervous?" she asked me.

"A little," I said.

"Don't be," Sophie said. She leaned into me

144

and put her hand behind my head and kissed me
again.

Her lips felt so delicate and vulnerable I was
almost afraid to kiss her back. Like a flickering
candle flame that might go out if you move too
suddenly.

After a while, she pulled away. "So let me get
this straight," Sophie said. "At Masthead. The night
of the formal. You smashed the dean's car through
the wall of the motel?"

"Yeah," I said. It didn't sound so heroic when
she put it like that. "It was an accident."

"What were you trying to do? Do you mind if we
go through this story just one time?" she said. "It's
like, I think I know the facts, but then there's parts
of it I don't know. "

I hesitated. Sophie took my hand. I closed my
eyes.

"I was going to—" I shrugged. I don't even know
what I'd been trying to do that night. "I was trying to
stop Sullivan from, you know, making you do something you didn't want to. I knew he'd been through
all the files of every girl in the class, so he could use
the information to blackmail you into doing what he
wanted."

I opened my eyes again. Sophie was nodding.
"Yeah," she said. "He's a real charmer."

"And Betsy Donnelly told me somebody had to stop him," I told her.

"So that's when you decided to drive the dean's car through the wall?" Sophie asked me.

I shrugged. "I guess I'm not a very good driver," I said.

Sophie laughed, like this was hilarious. It was the truth, though.

"I wasn't trying to drive the car through the wall," I explained. "I just lost control of it. I think I stepped on the gas instead of the brake."

"In the dean's Peugeot, Jonah?" Sophie said. "You couldn't have smashed up a Honda or something instead?"

"Anyway," I said. "After I smashed the car, everyone in the motel went screaming out of there. I saw you running off into the night."

"I saw you, too!" Sophie said. "That's where I know you from. That was you in the back of the cop car, wasn't it?"

Well, of course it was me, Sophie, who did you think it was? I thought. Did she really have no memory of me at all when I was at Masthead?

"I told them it was me in the motel room, not you and Sullivan. So you wouldn't get kicked out," I said.

"That's what I can't believe," Sophie said. "You

got yourself kicked out. For me. I mean you don't even know me!"

I smiled at her. "I'd like to," I said.

"Well," said Sophie, smiling. "I guess that's why we're here, isn't it?"

"Uh-huh," I said happily.

We kissed again, and this time it went on longer. It felt like we were kissing for hours. It felt like some wild dream and I didn't want to wake up.

"So," I said, like twenty-five years later when our lips were tired and we had to stop kissing. "What was in your file? The thing that Sullivan found out. The thing he was going to tell everybody?"

The second I said it, I knew it was a mistake. Sophie's body got all stiff and her eyes kind of shut off, like they were turning inward.

"I don't know," she said coldly. "I have no idea."

But from the way she said it, it sounded like she knew exactly what Sullivan had found out. It bugged me that she wouldn't tell me, after everything I'd done for her. But maybe I was pushing her too soon. She'd tell me when she was ready.

Sophie moved away from me. She looked nervous now. "Do you think this was a mistake, meeting here?"

"I don't know," I said. "I don't want it to be. It's

just strange to actually be sitting next to each other after all this time."

"If you only knew," Sophie said, and laughed quietly. There was something a little odd about her laugh. Like she was sharing a private joke with herself.

"If I only knew what?" I said.

"If you only knew how long I've been thinking about you," she said, but it didn't sound that that's what she'd been thinking.

"I've been thinking about you, too," I said. I leaned toward her and kissed her again, really softly, like I was afraid I'd scare her away.

Then Sophie reached her hand down to the hem of her sundress and in one motion she pulled it off over her head and there she was, sitting on the bed in a blue bra and some matching panties with a little blue satin rose on the waistband.

"Let's do it," she said. "Okay, Jonah? I think we should just go ahead and do it. I hope that's all right."

"That's fine," I said.

I pulled off my T-shirt and then I stood up and took my shorts and even my boxers off, and a second later I was totally naked, and Sophie was just watching me with this huge smile on her face.

She reached up and rubbed my chest and my

stomach and the small of my back. "You swim, don't you? You're like this big diving star or something," she said.

I shrugged. "Yeah, I guess."

"Your body is amazing," she said.

"Look who's talking," I said.

Then Sophie knelt on the bed and kissed my chest, over and over again, with these tiny little kisses, and each one was like a raindrop falling on the ocean. And then she turned me around and kissed my back and my shoulders. I spun around to pull her toward me, but she stopped me and reached around her back and took off her bra. A second after that, she stepped out of her panties.

And then, man, I can hardly even believe I'm writing this! I lay down and my head was on the pillow and Sophie kneeled over me, kissing my stomach and chest and neck. Then she lay on her back and I started kissing her. All over.

I felt like I was two people, the Jonah this was all happening to, and some other Jonah standing back and thinking, *Can you believe this? Are you remembering every single detail so you can remember this moment for your entire life?* I mean what if something happened like what happened to Pops's girlfriend? We could both be struck by lightning and never kiss each other the way we were kissing now.

Then Sophie sat up. "I have to go to the bathroom," she said. "I'll be right back, okay?"

I couldn't even speak. I just nodded.

Sophie picked up her little red purse and I watched her walk with it to the bathroom. When the door shut I closed my eyes, and I could still see her body, imprinted on the back of my eyelids.

She was gone for about five minutes. Then she came back. I could tell that while she was in the bathroom she'd brushed her hair and put on more lip gloss and basically put herself together once more. I couldn't believe she was trying to look even sexier for me. She was already sexy enough.

"Okay, Jonah," she said. "Let's do it."

I couldn't believe that after all these years I was about to lose my virginity to this amazing girl who thought I was a hero, even though I hadn't done anything more than drive a car into the side of a motel. But I felt like a hero then. And we'd been saving ourselves for each other. It was going to be perfect.

Sophie laid her head back on the pillow and her hair was streaming down over the sheets. I kissed her neck.

Just at that moment, a helicopter flew over the

hotel. Sophie's body tensed up and her face looked frightened. "Oh, no, the helicopters," she gasped.

She rolled off the bed and went to the window and peeked through the curtains. The sound of the helicopter was growing softer.

"What helicopters?" I said.

Sophie smiled in that weird way again. "Oh, nothing," she said. She came back and lay down on the bed and I rolled on top of her. But then she lifted her head and whispered, "No, Jonah. Kiss me some more."

So I slowly kissed my way down her body. I kissed the two little bones of her collarbone. I kissed the damp place between her breasts. I kissed around her belly button and down each of her legs to her toes. Everything was hushed and amazing.

This is getting too private to even write about, but I'd never done exactly this before so I was kind of making it up as I went along. Once, Sophie made this soft little cry, like the most private noise I've ever heard. I put my arm around her to let her know she didn't have to be afraid. And then I kept kissing her.

I couldn't believe any of this was happening. I felt like I was an astronaut walking in space. Everything was taking place in this incredibly silent, perfect place, far above the world, and everything was happening very slowly. And just like astronauts

hovering above the planet, Sophie and I were sur-
rounded by this radiant blue-white light.

Then I said, "Sophie, I love you."

And at that moment, she broke into tears.

For a few seconds I thought that maybe she was
so happy to be with me that she couldn't help crying. But the tears kept coming, and soon her body
convulsed in giant sobs. I was really worried. Had I
said something wrong?

"I'm sorry," I said. "It's okay."

"No," Sophie said. She wiped her eyes with the
back of her hands. "Let's just do it now, Jonah.
Please?"

She dropped her head back down on the pillow
again and squeezed my hand tight. "Please. I love
you," she whispered. But as she said it, she started
sobbing again.

I absolutely did not know how to handle this situation. I mean, there was Sophie, naked, asking me
to do something I'd been wanting to do since I first
saw her. And yet, how was I supposed to do that
when these huge tears were coming out of her eyes,
and her stomach was clenched in these gasping
sobs?

"Sophie," I said. "It's okay. You're safe."

She started crying even harder. I rubbed the
side of her face with my cheek.

"Go on," she said. "Jonah. Please."

I brushed the hair back from her face. "Sophie, I can't," I said. "Not while you're crying."

"I just cry before I do it." she said, "It's just this weird thing. Don't pay any attention."

This didn't sound right. She'd told me on the phone that she'd never done it with anyone. That she'd been waiting for me. Had she lied to me then? Or was she lying now? I was beginning to feel a little afraid of Sophie. There was something sort of raw about her, something out of control. She's definitely hard to pin down.

"I can't do it if you're crying," I said. "I don't want to do it."

"Please, Jonah," she whispered. "You just have to pretend I'm not crying. Use your imagination."

She pulled me toward her again. "Please," she said.

I pulled back. "No."

"Goddammit," she said, and she did this thing with her feet, like she kind of stamped them both back and forth on the bedsheets like a seal flapping its flippers. "It's not a big deal."

"Sophie," I said, and put my feet on the floor and cradled her head in my arms. "What's wrong?"

"Nothing's wrong. I don't want to talk about it."

"It's all right," I said. "You're totally safe. We

can stay here all night and talk. I'd much rather talk to you than—you know, do it."

"You'd rather talk? Jesus, Jonah, you're more screwed up than I am!" she said. She sounded fed up, like she was completely disgusted with me.

"I just want to know what's wrong," I said. "I don't mind listening."

"I don't want to talk about it," she said. "Okay?"

"It's really all right," I said. "You know I love you."

"Shut up!" she said, jumping up from the bed. "I said I don't want to talk about it! God, why does everything have to wind up being some great big stupid conversation?"

"Okay, then. We don't have to talk about it," I said. "Whatever. I'm just saying I'm glad to listen, if you want to talk or whatever."

"Right," she said, shaking her head. "Wow. Look at you. You're all sensitive."

The way she said this kind of pissed me off. "I don't know if I'm sensitive, but I'm happy to listen to you. It's just that I care about you, okay? Seeing you in tears doesn't exactly make me feel good." My voice had sort of an edge to it, and I suddenly felt totally out of control. I had no idea what was going to happen next.

"Well, I'm sorry if I hurt your feelings," Sophie said.

"It's not my feelings I'm worried about."

"I told you it's not a big deal. It's just this reaction I get," she said.

"It is a big deal," I said.

"Well, I'm not going to just pour it all out to you, Jonah," said Sophie. "As if you or anybody would ever, possibly get it." She pulled her dress on over her shoulders. "I must have been crazy."

"Wait," I said. "What are you doing?"

"Forget it," she said. "Just pretend I was never here, all right? That's what you should do."

She stepped into her sandals and grabbed her bra and panties in one hand and headed for the door.

"Stop," I said. "Please, Sophie. I'm sorry."

"Leave me alone," Sophie said.

I stood and took her by the hand. "Please wait," I said. "Sophie. Please."

"If you don't let go of me, I'm going to scream," she said, glaring at me like I was some stranger she'd never seen before.

"Sophie, I don't understand," I said.

"That's right. You don't. Now let me go, okay?"

The more I looked at her, it was like *she* was the stranger. Her face was convulsed in anger, her cheeks were red, and her eyes had this cold flame in them.

I couldn't think of anything else to do except let her go.

I sat on the edge of the bed and listened to her

footsteps going down the hallway. Then I went to the window and a moment later I saw her running across the parking lot, still holding her bra in one hand.

(Still Dec. 29, 8:30 A.M.)

I've been sitting at the restaurant now for almost two hours writing all of this down. Actually, I haven't been writing the whole time. I keep taking breaks and just staring off into space, thinking about what happened. I don't understand anyone at all.

And then . . . guess what? Just as I finished the last paragraph of the last entry, this hotel guy asked me if I was Mr. Jonah Black, and I said yeah, and I was afraid it was like hotel security or something about to throw me in jail—but instead this guy said, "I have an envelope for you." I followed him back to the front desk, and there it was—a fat white envelope.

So I got very excited, thinking it was going to be from Sophie and that she was going to explain what happened last night. Written on the envelope was my name in handwriting I didn't recognize.

I opened it up and there was a note inside.

GOOD LUCK WITH SOPHIE, JONAH. REMEMBER I'LL ALWAYS LOVE YOU TOO. —NORTHGIRL

PS: I KNOW YOU'RE OUT OF MONEY SO HERE'S
SOME CASH.

Paper-clipped to this note were five new hundred-
dollar bills.

I sat there holding the note in one hand. I couldn't
believe it! How did Northgirl know I was here? And
that I was short of money? And how did she get the
money to my hotel? Did she bring it herself? I looked
at the writing on the envelope again. It wasn't Posie's
handwriting, and it wasn't Thorne's or Honey's or anyone else I knew. Was it Sophie? It didn't seem likely,
especially after last night.

"Sir?" the concierge said. "I also have two
phone messages for you."

"Okay," I said. He handed me two pink slips. The
first said, *Jonah. Got lucky at UCF. I think I pledged
Deke last night, but I can't remember. I'll pick you
up at the front entrance today at four. Thorne.*

I liked how he thought he pledged Deke but he
couldn't remember. I think that's the kind of thing
you'd remember, if it happened.

I opened the second note. It was from Sophie.
*Jonah, I'm sorry. Please forgive me. Can I meet you
in Disney World today? Arch of Cinderella's Castle,
eleven A.M.? I promise I won't cry. I love you. Sophie.*

I stood there, completely amazed. She loves me.

So now I'm up in the hotel room, packing everything up. It's back to the Magic Kingdom for me.

I just hope I don't run into Posie again.

(Still Dec. 29, 12:30 P.M.)

Now I'm sitting at a table at the Diamond Horseshoe Jamboree, which is this kind of Wild West musical revue where you eat your lunch while everybody around you yells and sings cowboy songs.

Sophie wasn't at the castle at eleven.

I checked out of the hotel this morning and stored my bags at the front desk. Then I bought a bouquet of flowers from the gift shop and got the shuttle over here. I stood underneath the arch of Cinderella's stupid castle and waited for Sophie. I waited for fifteen minutes, I waited for a half hour, I waited for forty-five minutes. No Sophie. Just before noon I threw the flowers in the trash, totally disgusted. I walked over here to get something to drink and I've been sitting here ever since. I don't know what to do.

The thing is, I'm not ready to give up yet. Pops would be pretty disappointed in me if I gave up now. So would Thorne. And what about Posie? After all, she broke up with me so I'd be free to do this, hook up with Sophie. I owe it to Posie to get Sophie out of my system once and for all.

I have from now until four to meet up with her and see what's what. I don't even know if I'll see her. But if I do, I have a feeling I'm going to get burned again.

Dec. 30

Back in Pompano Beach.

Okay. I'm back in my room at Mom's house.

Now I have a broken arm.

I guess I should explain how I got the broken arm.

Before I do, though, I should describe the cast. It's from the middle of my forearm down to about the middle of my hand. Left arm.

It's got one signature on it, in red Magic Marker.

Marry me, Jonah. All my love forever.

The last few days have definitely been busy.

I'm probably not going to be able to write all this down in one sitting, so this might be a little disjointed.

Where was I? I guess I'd just left the Diamond Horseshoe Jamboree and I was trying to figure out where to go next. I had about three hours to kill before Thorne came to pick me up. I was kind of hoping I'd bump into Sophie, but Disney World is so big and so crowded, that was unlikely.

I was feeling pretty low. The past three days had just been so weird and sad and I didn't know whether I was glad I'd come or what. And everywhere I turned it looked like there were happy people, kids laughing, parents with their kids, couples my age holding hands.

Anyway, I was standing at the entrance to Fantasyland when suddenly I felt this hand on my shoulder.

I turned around. It was Sophie.

She was wearing a black jean miniskirt and a red T-shirt and her hair was just pouring down around her shoulders. She smelled like sweet sweat. Like flowers and sweat.

"Hi, Jonah," she said.

"Hi," I said.

She put her arms around me and hugged me hard. "I'm sorry," she said into my chest. "I am so sorry."

I felt myself melt. "It's all right," I said. "I just didn't understand what happened. I wanted to help you. Last night."

"Do you hate me?" she said.

"No, of course I don't hate you. I just want to help you. I—"

"Sshh," she said, and put one finger on my lips. "Let's forget last night, all right? I'm sorry I was so weird. What can I tell you? You're in love with a weird girl." Her eyes fell for a second. "I didn't mean to say that. I don't mean that you're actually, you know—"

"It's true," I said. "I am in love with you."

"Well, you shouldn't be," Sophie said. "You don't even know me."

"I want to know you," I said. "If you'll let me."

"Okay, Jonah," she said. "But first let's do it." She took my arm and we started walking through the Magic Kingdom.

I wasn't sure what she meant by that. Did she mean what it sounded like she meant? Like, actually have sex in Disney World?

There was something about Sophie that just fried my brains. I guess it should have been pretty clear to me, not only from the night before, but also from the way she said this, that Sophie was nuts. But it was like I was under some spell or something. All I wanted was to be with her. I didn't care how weird she was, or maybe her being so weird was what made me want her in the first place.

——— ■ ———

"I can't believe you're here," she said, taking my hand. "I thought I was never going to see you again."

She didn't try to do it with me right away. First we went to King Stefan's, which is this restaurant in Cinderella's Castle. I'd always heard you couldn't eat there without reservations. As it turned out, Sophie had reservations for two.

"How did you know you were going to find me?" I said.

"I didn't," she said.

We sat at a little table in the corner of King Stefan's and ate cheeseburgers and Cokes and French fries. We didn't talk for a while, we just sat there awkwardly and I felt like my head was going to burst open. I was afraid I was failing with her already, but I couldn't think of a thing to say. Anything I said I was sure would sound stupid.

"Do you like French fries, Jonah?" Sophie said after a while.

"Yeah. Sure. I love French fries," I said. Sure enough, I sounded stupid.

"I hate 'em," she said, eating hers. "I like onion rings a lot better." She giggled. "Hey, you know I used to know this guy who had onion rings for glasses."

"Yeah?" I said. It sounded like the first half of a joke, only she didn't say the other half.

"So when are you going home?" I said. It almost sounded like I was looking forward to her leaving.

"Today," said Sophie. She had some of her hair in her mouth and she removed it with one pinky. "I'm getting on a plane at six. What about you?"

"I have to be back at the hotel before four. Thorne's picking me up and we're driving home."

"Thorne," Sophie said, smirking. "You know he called me once? To tell me what you'd done?"

"Yeah," I said. In a way I owed this whole experience to Thorne. He was the one who first contacted Sophie.

"He thinks he's pretty hot stuff I guess. I don't know. Guys mystify me sometimes," she said.

I nodded. "Me too. Actually, everybody mystifies me."

"I'm sorry if I screwed up our big date," said Sophie.

"It's all right. Maybe this whole thing was stupid anyway," I said, swallowing hard. It felt like we were breaking up, even though we'd never been together.

"No, don't say that," Sophie said. She grabbed my hand, hard. "It wasn't stupid. It didn't work out exactly the way we wanted it to, but we had to do it. We had to meet. It's like we're linked, Jonah. It's like we're twins born to different parents or something. I don't know if I'm ever going to see you again or what, but I know my fate and yours are all wrapped up together. It wasn't just some random accident, you saving me last year. It was something you did because you had to. And I'm telling you this, Jonah Black. I'm going to save your life one day, too. I don't know how, or what I'm going to do, but I'm going to make a sacrifice for you some day, just like the one you made for me."

This was all pretty heavy. I just sat there holding her hand. I wanted to believe her, but something in me wasn't sure if I could trust anything she said anymore. And I kept looking at this half-eaten French fry on her plate with lipstick on it. When I first looked at it, it didn't look like lipstick—it looked like blood.

(Still Dec. 30, later)

Okay, had to stop and rest the ol' hand there. More on my afternoon with Sophie in Fantasyland, and how I wound up getting a broken arm.

We left King Stefan's and walked around with our

arms around each other through the crowds, through the lines. We stared at all the people, in the long lines for Cinderella's Golden Carousel and Snow White's Scary Adventures, and The Many Adventures of Winnie the Pooh and Dumbo the Flying Elephant. I don't know, it was like being on a ride itself, just walking through Fantasyland with Sophie. I felt like I was in some amazing dream and any second we would both disappear, but we didn't. I loved the feel of her waist, the way it fit perfectly in my hand. Every once in a while we'd stop and kiss and I'd close my eyes and hear all the sounds of Disney World all around me, coming from some distant planet.

"This is kind of like torture," I told Sophie, finally coming up for air.

"How come?" she said, looking into my eyes.

"Because it's like we get to be together for this one day and then we're apart again," I said. "I can't stand it."

"I know," said Sophie. "But it's still nice."

"Yeah," I said. "It is nice."

"Hey, Jonah, are you seeing anybody else?"

"You mean seriously?" I said. I thought about Posie. It was so weird—when I saw her at that UCF party, it was like she wasn't even real.

"No. Not really," I said.

"What's that supposed to mean?" she said.

"It means I broke up with someone a couple of weeks ago," I said.

"How come?" she said.

I shrugged. "I don't know. She knew about you, I guess."

Sophie's jaw dropped. "You broke up with someone over me?"

I nodded.

"Jonah," Sophie said. "You shouldn't have."

"Why not? I love you, don't I?" I said.

"Yeah," Sophie said. She looked down at her feet and smiled. "You do," she said.

"So how could I go out with somebody else if I'm in love with you?" I said. My voice was trembling. I was getting kind of emotional.

"Wow," Sophie said, looking up at me once more. "You're incredible."

She ran her fingers through my hair and kissed me again. "What about you?" I said. "Are you going out with anybody?"

"I don't know," she said. "You know how it is."

She looked up at It's a Small World as we started to walk by. It has all these bizarre little clocks spinning on the front of it. I wanted to ask Sophie what she'd meant when she said, "You know how it is," but she grabbed my hand and pulled me toward the entrance.

"Hey, let's go in here," she said. "I bet we could do it in here."

"Sophie," I said. "You're kidding."

"No, I'm serious," she said. "I know this guy who said he did it in It's a Small World. There's a place you can jump out of your boat. It's just behind the Eiffel Tower."

From inside the ride I could hear that song, that horrible song that goes on and on and on inside of It's a Small World. I wasn't sure I wanted to have sex while listening to that song. I wasn't sure I wanted to have sex in It's a Small World at all. I wasn't sure I wanted to go into It's a Small World even if we *didn't* have sex.

"No way," I said, but Sophie was running for the entrance and I had to follow her. There wasn't much of a line for It's a Small World. Probably with good reason.

Our little boat set sail into the ride. It was kind of like a little United Nations on heroin. Lots of little dolls from different countries danced around us and sang that repetitive song in their native tongues. I felt like I was going insane.

Then Sophie grabbed me and kissed me harder than she ever had before. "Jonah," she whispered. "I want to do it now."

"Now?" I said. I didn't like this one bit, but I

168

didn't want to stop either, in case it happened, and in case it was better than I could have hoped for.

Sophie pulled away from me and peered into the ride. "Listen," she said. "They're singing in French."

We floated into Gay Paree. Ahead of us was the Eiffel Tower, but there was no good way of getting to it. You can't just jump out of your boat. The Disney people have probably thought all this through. I mean, if people are going to jump out of a boat in It's a Small World and have sex anywhere, the most likely place to do it in is in France, right?

"We can't get there," I said, and I was kind of relieved.

"Jesus," said Sophie. "If you can't do it in Paris, then I don't know where you can do it."

We were drifting away from Paris now.

"Hey, Jonah, where are you going to college?" Sophie said.

"I don't know. It's a year away for me. I'm a junior, remember?" I reminded her.

"Yeah. I just wondered what your plans were," she said. "Hey, maybe you could go where I go, okay? I mean, that way we could be together."

"Where do you think you're going to go?" I said.

"I don't know. I'm applying to a bunch of places," she said.

"You think you're going to go to UCF?" I asked.

"Nah. The guys there are so lame," said Sophie. "I got into a fight with this one guy when I was there, and I had to hit him in the face with an ashtray."

I had this very clear picture of Sophie hitting someone in the face with an ashtray. There was definitely something scary about her.

"I don't know," she said. "Sometimes I think college just makes guys stupider."

Suddenly, at that exact moment, all the lights in It's a Small World went out. The boat we were in ground to a halt. The music stopped. The emergency lights flickered on.

"Whoa," Sophie said. "Somebody just pulled the plug!"

"Attention, please," said a calm, amplified voice. "There has been a temporary loss of power on this attraction. Please remain in your boat. We will have power restored in a moment."

"Jonah," said Sophie. "It's our chance!"

"Our what?" I said.

"Come on!"

She stood up and jumped from the boat onto this small platform. In the distance I could see the dim shape of the Eiffel Tower.

"Sophie," I said. "Get back in the boat!"

"Come on, Jonah," she said. "Take a chance, will ya?"

Knowing it was the wrong thing to do, I stood up and followed her.

We walked through the streets of Paris together. All around us in dim shadows were French bakeries and tiny little men with goatees and ascots drinking wine. Tiny little French girls with silk stockings stood frozen at the door to the Moulin Rouge. We cut behind some buildings and soon, there we were beneath the tower.

Sophie sat down and pulled off her panties. "Je t'aime," she whispered to me, and reached up and pulled me down to my knees.

We kissed and she reached down and undid my belt buckle. "Jonah," she whispered. Her eyes were closed. She lay back, pulling me down on top of her. "Jonah," she said again. "I love you."

In the distance I heard people on the ride, stuck in their boats, calling out for help.

Sophie sat up and pulled her T-shirt off over her head. A second later, her bra was lying beneath the Eiffel Tower.

I pulled my T-shirt off, too. Our chests rubbed against each other.

"This is definitely . . . something," I whispered. It struck me as one of the stupider things I'd ever said, but I didn't care.

"We're going to remember this our entire lives," Sophie whispered back.

Of course she was right. At least, I will.

I still had a condom in my wallet. It was one I'd bought to use with Posie, and never got to use. For just a second I felt bad, remembering Posie.

"Here," Sophie said, reaching for the condom. "Let me help."

Sophie ripped open the package. I stared up at the ceiling of It's a Small World. From where we were, behind the scenes, it looked like the backstage of a high school auditorium. Sophie pressed the unwrapped condom into my hand and kissed me.

"Okay," she whispered. "Now, let's do it."

"Okay," I said.

Sophie lay back with her arms over her head. I knelt beside her.

"Jonah," she moaned. "Please." Her eyes were closed.

I stayed like that for a second. Frozen. The whole world was echoing with weird, distant sounds. People on the ride were crying for help. Kids were making ghost sounds. Children were bawling.

"Jonah," Sophie said, and this time her voice caught in her throat. "Please." I looked down at her face. Tears were streaming from her eyes.

"Sophie," I said. "Are you okay?"

"Jonah, dammit," she said. "Just do it. Please. I want you."

Poor Sophie, I thought.

And then all the lights blinked on. The boats started to move. The French people started singing the It's a Small World song again.

I saw that I was kneeling on a piece of ply-wood with a pale, naked girl lying beneath me, lit by fluorescent lights. Sophie had a purple-and-yellow bruise on one leg I hadn't noticed before. Behind the tower was a pump of some sort, and the machinery started grinding into action once more.

It wasn't exactly romantic.

The condom felt cold and clammy in my hand. I dropped it on the plywood floor. I couldn't go through with it, not like this.

"Jonah," Sophie pleaded. "Please."

I just looked at her sad eyes and wiped one of her tears away with the side of my thumb.

"Are we going to do it or not?" Sophie said impatiently.

I shook my head.

"I don't think so," I said.

"Fine," she said, sitting up. "I thought you loved me."

She pulled her shirt on over her head. She pulled on her underwear.

"Sophie," I said. "Wait."

"Go to hell," she said, and dashed off. I pulled my clothes back on and took off after her. I ran through the streets of Paris, but I couldn't find her. Ahead of me were the boats from the ride, full of passengers. I couldn't see our boat anymore, but that's because it must have moved out of Paris by now. This couple was necking in front of me. I jumped into their boat.

"Hey," said the guy. He was absolutely huge, huger than Sullivan the Giant, huger than Lamar Jameson. "What do you think you're doing?"

"Sorry," I said. "I got lost."

"Get out of here," he growled. He looked like he wanted to eat me.

"Oh, Jeremy, leave him alone," said the girl. "He said he got lost."

"I said get out of my boat," said Jeremy. He stood up and started pushing me and a second later I fell out of the boat and went *splash* into the It's a Small World river.

I must have landed funny or something because for a second I thought I was going to drown. For a varsity diver that would have been pretty pathetic. I didn't drown, but by the time I got my head above water, another boat was bearing down on me. I surfaced just long enough to see this boat full of teenage girls looking at me with their eyes popping out of their heads.

Then they mowed me down. I heard the girls scream, and a noise like *ufff* as I fell down into the water. The sound, I realized, had come out of my own mouth.

I knew my arm was broken right away. There wasn't a lot of debate about it. I got my bearings and stood up, neck-deep in the water, and looked up to see yet another one of those stupid boats, again filled with screaming girls.

They sailed right over me, crushing my arm once more. I wondered if I was going to die that way in It's a Small World, getting run over again and again by teenage girls.

But then the ride stopped again, and the voice on the loudspeaker said, "Attention—please remain in your boats. This attraction is being paused for a moment while we assist one of our visitors."

Then these five huge guys showed up. They looked like the secret service. Disney cops.

"Okay, son," said the biggest one. "Let's get you out of the water."

I probably don't need to bring this up to date on much more than that. The big guys got me out of the water and they were pretty angry until they saw that my arm was broken. Then I was taken to a special clinic somewhere in Disney World through this series of underground tunnels to a doctor who set my arm. I guess I passed out somewhere along the way, which isn't surprising because my arm was killing me and I'd nearly drowned. Anyway, when I woke up, I was in an armchair in the Disney clinic wearing the cast. And it was signed, "Marry me, Jonah. All my love forever."

"Who signed it?" I asked the nurse.

"Your girlfriend," she said.

"Sophie?" I said. I described her. The nurse shook her head. "I don't know. I wasn't here when the girl came in." She looked at me like I was a naughty boy. "Did you propose to her?"

I wasn't sure what I'd done. "Yeah," I said for the hell of it. "I guess."

The nurse sighed. "That's so romantic!" Then she looked angry with me, in a motherly sort of way. "Of course, you're not supposed to leave the boats," she said. "You put yourself in real danger, Mr. Black. You could have gotten hurt!"

"I did get hurt," I said.

"Exactly," said the nurse, as if she were proud to have pointed out the obvious.

"What time is it?" I asked her.

"Three-fifteen," she said.

"Can I go?"

"Yes, of course."

She escorted me out of the clinic, and about a half hour later I was waiting in front of the Porpoise for Thorne, who for once in his life was not late. He pulled up in his Beetle and honked. When he saw my cast, he laughed.

"Good boy, Jonah," he said. "I knew you'd land her."

"I thought you'd be proud," I said.

"But jeez, man. Did you have to bust your arm to do it?"

"I guess I did," I said. I wondered if I should tell him what really happened.

"Man," said Thorne, shaking his head. "It's one thing after another with you."

"It's not a bad break," I said. "They said it can come off in a month."

He turned on the radio. "You think you'll get a scar out of it?"

"I don't think so," I said.

"Oh, well. Too bad." He looked over at the cast. *"Marry me?"* he said. "Is that what it says?"

I nodded. "That's what it says."

Thorne groaned. I thought you said you'd landed her!"

I felt my face growing hot. "I was going to," I said. "But she kind of flipped out."

"Marry you! Goddamn! I'll say she flipped out." He clapped me on the shoulder. "Don't worry. She'll get over it."

"I feel like I don't even know her any better than before I met her," I said miserably. "This whole trip was kind of a waste."

"Well," Thorne said. "I wouldn't go that far. I definitely made the most of it."

I didn't answer him. Suddenly, I couldn't wait to get home. Thorne pulled out onto the highway and revved up to eighty. He glanced at me. "So how'd you get the broken arm?" he said. "You gonna tell me the whole story, or what?"

As we made our way toward home, I told him the whole miserable story. Thorne laughed and laughed, like it was hilariously funny.

"That chick's been eating too many Cocoa Puffs," he said. "Where's she going to college anyway?"

"I don't know. She said she looked at UCF while she was here," I told him.

———— ■ ————

"Yeah? You know, I'm surprised she was even thinking about UCF," he said. "I mean the girls there are like, even crazier than she is. I was at this other party the first night we were here, and it was totally amazing. Seriously. I hooked up with like, every girl in the room, and they were all hot. Then this one chick takes me into this back room and she starts coming on to me and I'm thinking, *Hello, Kitty,* and just before we started really getting into it, guess what—Miss University of Central Florida starts to cry. I was so bored by that I just handed her some Kleenex and said, *Come on, Barbie, let's go party.* And the next thing you know, guess what—she hits me with this ashtray. I'm lucky I didn't wind up with a black eye. Dude, all I can say is, college girls are a little high-strung."

Didn't Sophie say she met some guy at UCF that she had to hit with an ashtray? But Sophie wouldn't be picking up guys like Thorne at a frat party, would she? I mean girls probably hit guys with ashtrays all the time at frat parties.

It wasn't Sophie he was about to sleep with, was it? Was it? And if she was at that party, what was she doing there when she was supposed to be with me?

I sat there for a long time, trying to muster the guts to ask Thorne to describe the girl who'd hit

179

him with the ashtray. But I didn't ask because I didn't want to know.

Anyway, I don't know what difference his description would have made to me. All I can see when I think of Sophie is that crazed, angry expression on her face. It makes me sad that she can even look that way.

Dec. 31, noon

Mom is down at the radio station re-editing some of her shows so they can be run as *The Best of Judith Black* because she wants to take next week off. She thinks I broke my arm while I was watching a football game at UCF. I told her I fell down the bleachers when the UCF tight end made a touchdown. She smiled when she saw what was written on my cast. "You're going to make so many new friends at college!" she said happily.

So it's just Honey and me at the homestead, and a little while ago the two of us were sitting around the kitchen table. Honey has been drinking cup after cup of coffee. She's trying to quit smoking, and instead has decided to become a caffeine addict.

I decided to tell Honey absolutely everything that happened when I was in Orlando. She's bound to find out anyway. I wish I hadn't though, because I didn't really like what she had to say about it.

"You want to know what I think, Liverwurst?" Honey asked me.

"I'm sure you're going to tell me anyway," I said.

"I think your Sophie is a wacko freak."

"You think so?" I said.

"I know so," said Honey. "Like, every time you were about to dive into the ocean blue, she bursts into tears? What's that all about?"

"I don't know. It is weird, though," I admitted.

"It's more than weird, big brother. It's nuts. If I were you, I'd be glad I got her out of my system," Honey said.

I just sat there thinking about this while she made herself some more instant coffee. She shook the crystals into a glass and added hot water from the tap.

"Oh, no," she said, looking at me. She picked up a pencil and started wapping the eraser end against the table. "You're not."

"I'm not what?"

"You're not over her."

I sighed. "I don't know what I am."

"Oh, you moron," she said. "You're more in love with her than ever, now, aren't you?"

I shrugged again.

She snapped her fingers in front of my eyes. "Snake Lips. Wake up. You better get over this girl. Can't you see she's out of her mind?"

"She's not out of her mind. She just needs someone who will listen to her," I said.

"Yeah, like a goddamned psychiatrist."

I shrugged. As far as I was concerned the conversation was over.

"Jonah." Honey took my hand and squeezed it hard. "You don't mind if I call you Jonah, do you?"

"If you let go of my hand you can."

She didn't let go of my hand. "I am trying to tell you something, so I am holding your little hand so you will pay attention. Are you paying attention?"

I nodded. Honey squeezed my hand even harder. It hurt.

"This girl of yours from Maine?" she said.

She leaned very close to my ear as if to whisper. Then she shouted at the top of her lungs. *"She's a goddamned psycho!!!!!!!"*

"Ow," I said.

"Like, *hello*??? Might it have been more obvious if she had a sign around her head that says, I'M A WALKING PSYCHO? Like, somehow she convinces you to do her inside of It's a Small World, which is probably like, this big insane fantasy she's had all her life—having sex to that song. Then *Miss Nutcase* starts bawling, and takes off, leaving you inside the ride to break your arm. Then she signs your cast and *asks you to marry her* while you're unconscious. Then she disappears again. Jesus Christ, kid, my advice? RUN, DON'T WALK!!!!"

Honey let go of my hand. "I hope you don't think I'm being too subtle."

I rubbed my sore fingers. "I know she's a little different," I said. "But she said something else, too. She said she owed me—like our fates are intertwined somehow, and since I did her this big favor last year someday she's going to do me a favor, too. Like, to pay me back."

"Androcles and the lion," Honey said.

"What?"

"Androcles and the lion. An Aesop's fable. You know it, Pinhead. The lion with a thorn in his paw, guy saves him, later guy is in the Colosseum, lion decides not to eat him. It's a classic."

"Sophie's not a lion," I said.

"Maybe not, but she's not just 'a little different,' either. I'm telling you, Frankfurter, she is one sick chick. Forget about her," advised Honey. "Hey, even if your fates are intertwined, or whatever. The hell with her. There are a lot of girls whose fates you can intertwine with. The world's full of them."

"I don't know. I guess I'm kind of haunted by her or something," I said.

"*Of course* you're haunted by her. That's just what she wants, Pork Chop! I've seen this act again and again, that's what these little psycho chicks want—for you to be thinking about them all the time. She's got no intention of having sex with anybody, all she does is get people right up to the pearly gates and then she starts crying. As long as you're thinking about her, she can keep treating you like dirt. Listen, Clammy, if she really thought your fates were connected, she wouldn't keep taking off on you. It's an act! And what about the fact that when you asked about other guys she didn't give you a straight answer? I know it's hard because you're a little squish-head, but if you don't put this psycho-babe behind you, you're going nowhere fast. And that would be seriously lame-o. You know why? Because that chick Sophie is a great big FAKE."

Honey finished her coffee, then got up and shook more crystals into her glass. She ran it under the hot water tap. "Hey, you want some coffee?" she said. "As long as I'm up?"

I just sat there shaking my head. The horrible thing is that I'm pretty sure Honey is right. I guess I'm going nowhere fast.

(Still Dec. 31, 3:35 P.M.)

I just got back from a bike ride around Pompano. I went over to the beach and climbed up the lifeguard tower. I was kind of hoping Pops Berman would be there, but he wasn't. I biked over to Niagara Towers and rang his bell. No answer.

I'm beginning to have a bad feeling about Pops.

(Still Dec. 31, later)

Just got off the phone with Thorne. The weird thing is, it's New Year's Eve and I don't have any plans. Everyone's doing their own thing tonight. Thorne is going off to some party at Elanor Brubaker's house. He invited me, but I said no. Honey is going to hook up with Smacky Platte, who's had a relapse. And Mom and Mr. Bond—I mean *Robere*—are having dinner at the Lobster Pot. They invited me, too, but I politely declined.

Which leaves me on my own. I still feel pretty lousy about Pops. It's as if I've let him down somehow.

I also feel kind of lousy about myself. I've spent the last month in this blue haze, like living in a land of make-believe. I mean I don't think it's wrong to spend your time thinking about a girl, especially if you think you might love her. But Honey really is right about Sophie. She hasn't been straight with me. I want to help her, I want to be her friend, but somehow the more I get to know her, the less I know her. And maybe that's just the way she wants it.

So now I'm lying here watching the sun reflect off of the clouds. I just picked up the telescope and looked at a single lonely cloud moving across the horizon. It made me feel even more sad. But suddenly I realized that the whole time I was watching this distant cloud and getting all melancholy about it, the obvious thing is staring me right in the face. The most important thing is not that stupid cloud, it's this telescope Posie gave me. Posie, who really does love me, not because I did her a favor once, but because she knows me. Because she knows who I am, and has loved me my whole life.

Now I know what I'm doing tonight. I'm spending New Year's Eve with Posie.

(Still Dec. 31, 5:15 P.M.)

Except Posie isn't home.

AMERICA ONLINE
INSTANT MESSAGE FROM NORTHGIRL999,
12-31, 7:32 P.M

NORTHGIRL999: Hi Jonah!

JBLACK94710: Hi Northgirl.

NORTHGIRL999: How's it going?

JBLACK94710: Truthfully? Lame. I think I've made a huge mistake.

NORTHGIRL999: Let me guess. U spent a few days with your friend Sophie and now you realize she's a phlegmball.

JBLACK94710: Something like that.

NORTHGIRL999: I'm sorry you broke your arm.

JBLACK94710: You know about that?

NORTHGIRL999: Hey, stupid. Who do you think signed your cast?

JBLACK94710: What?

NORTHGIRL999: "Marry me Jonah. All my love forever."

JBLACK94710: Wait, that was you? You signed my cast? Hey Northgirl, this isn't fair. WHO ARE YOU?????

NORTHGIRL999: That's for me to know and you to find out.

JBLACK94710: But when am I going to find out?

NORTHGIRL999: You really want to know?

JBLACK94710: Yes please.

NORTHGIRL999: Probably never.

JBLACK94710: Damn. I thought Sophie signed it.

NORTHGIRL999: Are you kidding? Sophie was halfway back to

Canada, or wherever she's from before you even got out of It's a Small World.

JBLACK94710: This is so creepy. It's like you're some sort of guardian angel.

NORTHGIRL999: Yeah, I can see how you would think it's creepy. But it's not impossible to figure out who I am. I'm someone you see all the time. You just never take me seriously. That's what makes me invisible, you moron. The fact that you won't see me.

JBLACK94710: I'm sorry I haven't guessed. You promise me you're not Sophie? Posie? Honey? Mom? Thorne? Pops Berman?

NORTHGIRL999: Pops who?

JBLACK94710: Never mind.

NORTHGIRL999: I'm not any of those people.

JBLACK94710: Then I'm an idiot.

NORTHGIRL999: That gets clearer every day. Hey, hope that money came in handy.

JBLACK94710: Hey, yeah, that's another thing. Five hundred bucks? Where did you get five hundred bucks?

NORTHGIRL999: "Hey, yeah, that's another thing."

JBLACK94710: How am I supposed to thank you? What am I supposed to do about you?

NORTHGIRL999: Take me seriously.

JBLACK94710: How can I take you seriously?

NORTHGIRL999: By figuring out who I am.

JBLACK94710: How can I do that?

NORTHGIRL999: Yeah, well. I guess it's like some big mystery then. So what are you doing for New Year's Eve?

JBLACK94710: I don't know. I was going to try to find Posie and tell her I'm an idiot and that I'm sorry but now I can't find her. Nobody's home at the Hoffs'.

NORTHGIRL999: Well I wish you would spend New Year's with me instead.

JBLACK94710: I wish you'd let me.

NORTHGIRL999: No, no. You have to prove yourself worthy first.

JBLACK94710: HOW CAN I PROVE MYSELF WORTHY IF I DON'T KNOW WHO YOU ARE?

JBLACK94710: HELLO?

[Northgirl999 is not currently signed on.]

(Still Dec. 31, 10:35 P.M.)

I'm alone in the house, New Year's Eve, and feeling pretty down.

I admit to having attempted to call Sophie in Kennebunkport, but there's no answer at their house, either. It's like everyone I know in the universe has just disappeared.

Of course, after abandoning me in It's a Small World it's kind of up to HER to contact *me*, right? If she's going to do me this big favor someday, you'd think she might start by saying, "Hey, sorry I acted like such a freak." But no.

Oh. I got a phone call from Thorne about an hour ago. He was still trying to get me to go to this party with the St. Winnifred's crowd tonight. But I'm definitely not in the mood. I'd probably run into that girl Molly Beale again, and she'd accuse me of being full of crap for running out on her at that UCF party. Maybe she's right, too. I should have ditched Sophie and stayed at the party. Molly and I could be hanging out by the pool right now. I could show her my dives. I'm not sure I could handle Molly right now anyway—she's pretty intense.

Just before we hung up Thorne said, "Hey, Jonah. Good news. I talked to my dad. He's really looking forward to you working on the *Scrod* next summer."

Happy New Year to me. I guess I'll just go watch the ball drop on TV like a loser.

Jan. 1, noon

This has to be one of the last entries in this journal. Not only because I'm almost out of pages, and not only because it's a new year, but because of what happened last night. I think I should stop writing stuff down, unless I want to go down in history as the lamest creature alive.

Here goes.

At about eleven forty-five I got on my bike and decided, the hell with everything, I'll just go for a long ride. Get a little perspective, some exercise.

It was a beautiful night. I could see all the stars. There was Orion, and the Little Dog, and the Twins. Over beneath the handle of the Big Dipper was Arcturus, smoking his pipe.

Thorne and I were in Cub Scouts when we were ten, and we learned the names of the constellations at a winter bonfire. My dad taught us. That's one of my better memories of Dad.

Anyway, I turned down Route 1 and went past the golf course, and threaded my way around the old baseball park. I was riding one-handed because of the cast. I remembered the long summer days playing baseball in that park, standing in the outfield, watching Posie hit home runs over my head.

I rode past the amphitheater and down along 8th Street, past the little houses, all lit up blue by television lights. Everything seemed very quiet and I thought about all the people sitting on their sofas, watching the ball drop at the exact same time.

And then I went north and there was the Goodyear blimp, all lit up by spotlights, sitting in the hangar. I stopped the bike for a second and just looked at the blimp, and suddenly I started laughing and laughing.

I mean, if somebody had walked past they would have thought, *Here's some kid with a broken arm who's lost his mind.* But I couldn't help it. It's that stupid blimp. It was just the dumbest thing. So useless. And suddenly everything I'd been through—even

breaking my stupid arm in It's a Small World—
especially that—seemed completely hilarious.

So I rode back across to Federal Highway
along Copans Road, and then I cruised over to the
ocean. Once again I climbed the lifeguard tower
and I thought, *I have to find out what happened
to Pops Berman.* I could really use his advice
right now.

I watched the stars some more. There was a big
bright one in the Twins, and I knew it was some
planet, but I wasn't sure which one.

And that's when I realized I already knew
exactly what Pops would tell me to do if he was
there. He'd say, "Go walk the doggy, Chipper!"
That made me laugh some more. I'm turning into a
real nutcase.

So I got back on the bike and rode up to
Lighthouse Estates and pulled over in front of the
Hoffs' house. Posie's car was there and I saw her as
I pulled into the driveway, with her head out her
bedroom window, looking up at the stars. She didn't
see me, because she was just staring up at the
heavens. I felt so happy seeing her there, I wanted
to shout out loud.

But I was feeling kind of sneaky and silly so I
crept around the side of the house and snuck in
through the dog door so I could surprise her. I

remembered sneaking in that doggy door when we were kids, back when Posie had a dog called Pretzel. It seemed like a long time ago.

No one else was home—I could tell because the house was very dark and still. I got to the top of the stairs and I thought I heard a soft sound and I thought maybe Posie was crying. I'd broken up with her and left her alone on New Year's Eve. I felt terrible. But I was about to make it all up to her.

I pushed open the door and there she was. My Posie. My real love. Rolling around on the bed with Lamar Jameson.

A second later I was on my way out the dog door again. Except this time I got stuck. Posie and Lamar were going to come down the stairs any second and yell at me and ask me what I thought I was doing, and I wondered why I thought it was necessary to go out the dog door on the way *out,* when I could have just used the stupid door. Pretzel hadn't been a very big dog in the first place, and I was seriously wedged.

While I was trying to squirm my way out, I thought about Sophie, lying on my hotel bed, crying. And I thought, *What a sad world it is.* Full of heartbreak and who the hell knows what else.

And just like that I was out the door. I got back on my bike and I looked back up at the house. No one was coming after me. No one even knew I was alive.

So I came back home and took off my clothes and lay down on top of my bed, and then I felt this thing digging into my back. I rolled over and there was the Polaroid I'd taken of myself before Christmas. My last day as a virgin.

I still look exactly the same.

Okay, here's what happened last night while I was lying in bed.

I heard a familiar sound. A boat out on Cocoabutter Creek, the engine shutting down, then the rope going over our dock, and her feet coming up the lawn. The tap on my door.

I turned.

"Yo, Jonah," said Posie. "Come on. Let's take a ride."

I got up and on the way out the door I grabbed the telescope.

I sat down in the cockpit next to Posie and she looked over at my broken arm and read where it said *Marry me, Jonah*. She just shook her head and laughed. Then she started up the motor and we cast off. We moved quietly through the canals, past all the sleeping houses. Posie was wearing her red bikini, a blue fleece jacket, and a Marlins cap backward on her head. I don't know how many times Posie has shown up at my house late at night in her boat and said, "Come on, Jonah, let's take a ride." Too many times to count.

We didn't talk. We just followed the canal out to Lighthouse Point and then out into the ocean.

There were so many things I wanted to say to her. Like how Sophie wasn't what I'd hoped or expected. She was like a witch, disappearing into cobwebs. Or that I'd seen Posie at the UCF party but I didn't say hi because I was ashamed. Or that I saw her in the Haunted House with her little sister, Caitlin, and she looked so happy. And how later, when I saw my own reflection at the end of the ride, I didn't even recognize myself. That I'd seen her with Lamar.

But I didn't say any of those things. I just sat there listening to the outboard roaring, and watching the lights from shore growing smaller and smaller.

Then I got a big lump in my throat because the last time we came out to the ocean like this was when it all started between us. That was the night Posie and I first said that we were in love and we almost had sex. I wished I hadn't broken up with her. I wished I'd realized how perfect she is for me.

Anyway, we got about a half mile offshore, and the ocean was very calm and the stars were bright. Posie cut the motor and we drifted there. She reached under her seat and handed me a thermos. It was lemonade. Sour and sweet at the same time.

"So you're getting married, Jonah?" she said.

I shrugged and shook my head. "No. Not yet."

She took the thermos back and took a swig. "That girl turned out to be a disappointment, huh?"

I looked at the horizon. There were some cruise ships way out in the distance. I could hear music.

"Not really a disappointment. Just not what I'd expected. She was kind of strange," I said. "It's like I didn't get to meet her at all. She kept slipping out of my hands or something."

Posie nodded. "Uh-huh."

"What do you think is up with that?" I said.

"What do I think? I don't know." She rubbed my shoulder with her hand. "Maybe she doesn't want you to have her. Maybe she just wants you to want her."

Leave it to Posie to make it all totally clear, in like, a single sentence.

"Well, I don't want her, not anymore. I'm through with her. She's nothing but trouble," I said.

Posie laughed out loud. "You tell 'em, Jonah!"

"What?" I said, indignant.

"C'mon, Jonah, who do you think you're talking to? You're totally in love with her. Listen to you. You're worse off than before!"

"I'm not in love with her," I said. I drank some more lemonade. "Or, I don't know, maybe I am. But I know she's really screwed up. I just have to cut her loose. You know what she did? Every time I was about to have sex with her, she started crying."

Posie kind of flinched at this, as if she was surprised.

"That's weird," she said. "That's really weird."

"So I just have to draw a line, not allow her to take over my life anymore. I need to get back to normal," I said. I was trying to convince myself of this. I just need to get back to normal.

Posie drank more lemonade.

"Guess you heard about Lamar and me going out now," she said.

I nodded. Yeah, I'd heard about it all right.

There was a long silence. I wasn't used to long silences with Posie. It felt weird.

"So you guys are pretty tight now I guess?" I said. "You and Lamar?"

Posie just nodded. "He's pretty great," she said.

My shoulders fell. I felt like crying.

Posie rubbed my shoulder some more. "Poor Jonah," she said.

"Oh, I get what I deserve," I said. "I'm such an idiot."

"No, you're not," Posie said. "You're not. And you know what, you don't get what you deserve, Jonah. You deserve to be happy. You really do. You're a great guy. You care about people. You're aware of things that most guys don't even know they should know."

"Lucky me," I said.

"Yes, lucky you. And lucky for the right girl, someday," Posie said. "I mean, when you meet her."

Again it got quiet. I looked out at the cruise ships for a while. I would love to take a cruise with Posie. I can just see her, water-skiing in her red bikini off the end of the ship, waving to me while I drink cocktails with umbrellas in them and watch her from up on deck. Sophie comes up behind me and slips her arms around my waist.

"Mmmn," she says. We are so relaxed we don't have to speak in words.

"Mmmn," I whisper back to her, leaning my cheek against her. Her skin is warm and brown and smells of coconuts. We've been at sea a long time.

"Jonah?"

I turned back to Posie.

"I don't suppose you and Lamar are thinking of

breaking up anytime soon?" I said with a sad smile.

Posie smiled back. "Sorry, Jonah. You made your choice."

"Yeah, but it was the wrong choice, I think," I said lamely.

Posie started the engine. "C'mon, Jonah," she said. "Let's head home."

She headed the boat back to Lighthouse Point, and as we drew closer I saw all the twinkling lights of Pompano Beach. It looked like someplace you'd want to go home to. I'm glad I live here.

A little while later Posie dropped me off at the dock in back of our house, and she kissed me. The kiss went on for a long time. It felt like a friendly kiss or a good-bye kiss or something. It wasn't a come-on kiss, it was sad.

"Thanks for the telescope, Posie," I said.

"You're welcome. You never know," she said. "One of these days you might want to get a good look at some heavenly bodies."

"I already have," I said.

Jan. 5

I'm just about to run out of pages in this thing, but I have to write this one last entry.

Today I was on my bike and I went up to the little record store on Federal Highway and I spent a while in there just looking at CDs and sort of looking at the girls looking at the CDs, and there was this one girl who seemed sort of familiar, although I didn't really get a good look at her at first. She was sort of sneaking these glances at me out of the corner of her eye. So I was like, hey, this is kind of cool. But I didn't want to act like a stalker and walk over to her and say something stupid, so I just turned my back on her and started looking through the funk CDs. Old stuff like Parliament. I guess I was hoping she'd think that was cool, that I was into funky music.

Except when I turned around she wasn't in the store anymore.

So this kind of bummed me out because I figured, once again I've totally misjudged what a girl is thinking. I left the store without buying anything and I went outside, just in time to see this giant Ford Expedition totally crushing my bike beneath its tires. At first I thought I was imagining it, but no. It was happening for real.

The driver stopped the car after about two seconds. He was making a turn off of Federal Highway onto 25th Street, and I guess my bike was too close to the curb or something because he must have just nicked the back tire with his fender, which made the bike fall over and then he couldn't help but run over the whole thing. He stopped the Expedition and I went rushing over, about to yell my head off.

But the person in the car wasn't a guy at all. It was the girl from the record store. And I wondered, wait, did she crush my bike with her SUV just so she could talk to me? I mean, it's devious, but it's not out of the question. I could imagine myself doing that. It's not beyond the realm of possibility.

The girl was standing there looking at the bike

when I walked up behind her. She glanced at me. "Is this your bike?" she said.

"Yeah. Well, it was," I said.

"Sorry."

I wanted to yell at her, "Hey, you should look out where you're going. What are you, stupid?" but instead I started staring at her because I realized I knew her.

"You're Jonah Black, aren't you?" she said.

"Yeah."

"I'm Molly. From that party at UCF. You ditched me, remember?" she said.

"I didn't ditch you," I said.

"You did indeed. We were going to sit down on that zebra-skin couch and converse. One of the topics of discussion as you'll recall was whether or not guys are completely full of crap. As I believe you'll agree you turned out to be that night?" she said.

She talked like she was a robot or something, except that she seemed to mean everything she was saying. I didn't know what to make of her. She was cute, though. My eyes fell to her chest, and I remembered what she'd said at the party about looking at her boobs. I blushed and looked up.

"Is that why you ran over my bike?" I said.

"Why? Because you ditched me at the party?"

She laughed loudly. "You know, I wish I had. That would have been crafty."

"So you didn't?" I said, still a little suspicious.

"No. I just screwed up. I'm sorry. I kind of suck at driving, actually. I'm always running stuff over. Crashing into things." She shrugged. "You want a ride?"

So she tells me she's a terrible driver and that she's always crashing into things, and then she wants to know if I want to ride around with her? It didn't sound like a good offer. And yet, it seemed like it had all kinds of possibilities.

"Sure," I said. I told her where I live.

"Welcome aboard," said Molly.

We tossed the remains of my bike in the back and then jumped in the cab.

"What do you think of this car—do you think it's a bullshit car?" Molly asked me, starting it up. On the stereo, a girl was singing in French. Molly turned it down.

"Well, I don't know," I said. "It's not what I'd expect you to drive."

"It's my father's," Molly explained. "And yes, it *is* a bullshit car. It's a giant off-road vehicle, as if there's anyplace in Florida that *isn't* paved. Is there a single reason for anyone to own or drive a car like this, other than that they are on a total ego trip? No, there isn't."

——— ■ ———

Molly had overestimated her driving skills. She was actually the worst driver I'd ever been in a car with. We were weaving all over the place, and she ran a red light. That on top of crushing my bike. I was actually glad we were in an SUV at that moment, just so there'd be some protection when we hit whatever it was Molly was going to hit next.

"Hey, get out of my way!" Molly shouted, veering around a woman clutching her small child's hand. This was at a crosswalk.

Seeing how Molly drives makes me feel like I should have passed my driving test, even if I did hit someone. I didn't do it on purpose. I mean if someone walked in front of Molly's car, she'd probably just speed up and mow them down.

"So why did you ditch me at the party, Jonah?" Molly said. "I was pretty browned off at you."

Browned off? Who says things like browned off? I shrugged. "I just had to get out of there."

Molly jammed on the brakes of the SUV. All of the tapes and CDs on the dash went sailing into the backseat. I was afraid she'd run over something again.

"You want to get out? You want to walk home?" she snapped.

"What?" I said.

"Don't lie to me, okay? That's what I liked about

you in the first place, that you weren't full of crap. You don't know me, I don't know you, we can keep it that way if you want. But if you want to be friends, we tell the truth. About everything. Okay?"

I nodded. She started driving again.

"Is that what you want?" I said. "To be friends?"

"Well, I think so. Assuming you don't screw it up with a bunch of crap," Molly answered.

"You don't have a lot a friends, do you?" I said. I realized this just as I said it.

"Do I have a lot of friends? Interesting question, Jonah Black. No, I do not. I drive most people crazy. Why do you think that is?"

I started laughing. Then Molly looked at me, and laughed, too.

"Because you're obsessed with whether or not things are bullshit?" I said.

Molly nodded. "Exactly," she said. "See, I knew you and I were going to get along."

I like her, I decided. She's a little bit nuts, but she's funny. She isn't like anybody I've ever met before. Although I have to admit, she kind of intimidates me.

"But first you have to tell me why you left that party," Molly insisted. "I went to the Little Girls' Room and voilà—you were gone."

"I saw somebody I knew," I admitted. "I saw

someone at the party I didn't want to see me."

"And what would her name be?" Molly asked.

"Posie," I said.

"And you're in love with her?" Molly said.

"I don't know," I said. Molly looked at me, and raised one eyebrow.

"Please, don't jam the brakes on again, okay? It's the truth. I don't know what I think about her anymore. I just didn't want her to see me right then," I said.

At that second I caught a glimpse of the ocean, the sun turning it silver, and I had this intense flash, a crystal-clear memory of the night a few months back when Posie and I had gone out in her boat to look at a school of phosphorescent jellyfish. Posie turned off the motor and we just floated on the ocean, listening to the sound of the waves and the wind, and looking at the jellyfish suspended all around us.

"You're a real daydreamer, aren't you, Jonah Black?" Molly said.

I was embarrassed. "How can you tell?"

"Well, let's just say it was a good guess. You think we can be friends, you and me? A chick who only wants people to tell the truth, and a guy who lives in his head most of the time?"

"Who says I live in my head most of the time?" I said.

Molly smirked. "Don't play games with me. I can read you like the dictionary."

"I don't know," I said.

"Stop saying that, you're getting boring."

"But I really don't know if we can be friends," I said. "You want me to tell the truth, don't you? I thought that was your big thing."

"Oh, forget it," she said. "Why don't you just make up something nice? Tell me what I want to hear. Be interesting."

"Okay," I said. "Yeah. I think we can be friends."

Molly smiled happily. I noticed her eyeteeth were pretty long, for a girl.

"Good," she said.

We pulled up in front of Mom's house. Mom was sitting there on the front steps, reading the mail.

"Home again, home again, jiggety jig," said Molly.

"Thanks for driving me home," I said.

"Yeah, well. Sorry about the bike," she said. "Hey, this is what I propose. The two of us take the afternoon, drive around for a while. Get to know each other better? I'm really not such a bitch, actually. Although I am a pretty bad driver."

Mom was looking up at the car idling on the curve.

"Yeah," I heard myself say. "Sure. Let me just say hi to my mom first, all right?"

Molly smiled. "Sure," she said. "You talk it over with Mom. I'll dump the flattened, twisted remnants of your bike on the lawn. Sound good?"

I said okay, and climbed out of the Expedition. "Hi, Mom," I said. Molly opened the back of the SUV.

"Hi, Jonah," she said. "Here, you have a letter." She handed it to me.

Molly put the pieces of my bike in the driveway.

"Who's your little friend, Jonah?" Mom said.

"Oh, Mom, this is Molly."

"Hello, Molly," Mom said, standing up to shake hands. "I'm Judith Black."

I looked at the letter in my hand. *It was from Sophie.*

"Judith Black? Not the Judith Black on the radio?" said Molly.

"That's me," Mom said proudly.

"Oh, dear!" Molly said with a sort of grimace.

"What do you mean by that, Molly? You sound upset," Mom said.

"Well, Mrs. Black, I genuinely don't wish to be disrespectful, since you've clearly worked hard to get where you are. But I'm afraid your radio show is just totally bogus." Molly smiled, as if she truly hated having to talk this way. "And your book, *Hello Penis, Hello Whatever*? It's just full of misinformation. I'm sorry. I know this must seem rather rude."

Mom was just standing there. No one had ever talked to her that way before. Hell, no one ever called her "Mrs." anymore. They just went along with her whack story about being "Dr." Judith Black.

I opened the letter from Sophie.

"I was wondering," Molly went on, "—and you should simply tell me if you're not comfortable answering this question—but I'm really curious whether you actually have any psychological training whatsoever? I mean are you an MSW? Have you done any graduate work in counseling or therapy? Have you ever studied human sexuality? If so, it's just surprising to me, given—"

"Bup, bup, bup," said Mom, holding her hand out to indicate that Molly should stop talking now. "I'm sorry, but I don't want to play the Honesty Game with you right now. All right?" She put her fingers to her forehead, as if she was getting a headache.

"The Honesty Game?" Molly said. "Is that what you call it?" She shook her head. "See, I don't think that honesty is a game. I think that's a very odd thing to say, Mrs. Black. If you don't mind my speaking so freely."

"Bup, bup, bup," Mom said again.

"Okay," Molly said. "Well, whatever." She started walking toward her car. "I'll meet you in the Expedition, Jonah Black."

The letter from Sophie was written in this thin spidery writing, like it had taken a lot of energy to write it.

Dear Jonah, it read.

> *You probably don't want to hear from me but you're the only person in the world who can help me. I'm in this place called Maggins, which is basically a mental institution. My father has dumped me here and they won't let me call or write anybody. My friend Becky is being discharged and she says she'll try to put this in the mail to you. I'm sorry I was so horrible to you, but I'm all screwed up. I'm sorry I'm sorry I'm sorry. I ought to have told you everything about me but I was afraid if you knew the truth you wouldn't like me anymore. Please come and see me, Jonah, I am totally desperate. This place is in Pennsylvania, about a mile from Masthead. You saved me once, and now I need you to save me again. I know I said that next time I'd do you a favor but instead it looks like I'll have to do you two favors when I get the chance. Please come, Jonah. I really do love you. I want to be with you. Maybe if you find out who I really*

*am it won't be so hard for me. I just don't
have any experience with people actually
knowing me. Please come, Jonah, you're
my only hope.*

> *Love always,*
> *Your Sophie*

I stood there in Mom's front yard looking at the
letter. I couldn't believe it, Sophie in Maggins! She
didn't have to tell me where it was, everybody at
Masthead knew about it. It was a terrible place, the
kind of place they sent you if they didn't think
you'd be coming back out again. When we used to
go past it, we'd always look the other way. It was a
big old nineteenth-century stone building that
looked like the Haunted House in Disney World.
Even the *outside* gave me the creeps.

I imagined myself flying back up to Pennsylvania,
going down some long corridor of Maggins with all
these rooms with bars on the windows, hearing all
these girls crying. Sophie reaches her hand out to
grab my shirt and pulls me to her, kissing me hard.

"Get me out of here, Jonah," she says.

Then I thought about what an idiot Sophie had
made of me in Disney World. I'd promised myself I
was going to put her behind me. I wasn't going to
spend the rest of my life helping her out.

But that was before I knew how much trouble she was in, or how troubled she was.

I stood there for what seemed like forever, trying to figure out what I was going to do.

Molly honked the horn of her car. Her hair fell from behind her ear.

"Hey, Jonah," she called. "You coming?"

———■———

WILL JONAH AND MOLLY GET IT ON?
WILL JONAH EVER FIGURE OUT WHO NORTHGIRL IS?
WILL JONAH ANSWER SOPHIE'S CALL FOR HELP?

FIND OUT IN THE NEXT INSTALLMENT OF
JONAH BLACK'S JOURNAL . . .

The Black Book
[DIARY OF A TEENAGE STUD]

VOL. IV: FASTER, FASTER, FASTER

———■———